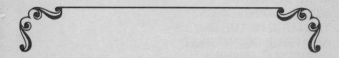

"I asked you to kiss me, sir." Holly was beside the desk, nervously rearranging the inkwell and blotting paper. "And don't say you don't wish to, for I know otherwise. You're always so careful not to show your emotions, but I can tell by how you stared at my ... person when we fenced, and tonight, when you were sitting next to me on the music bench, I know you felt the warmth when our thighs touched."

"With all your experience with men, how do you know that means I want to kiss you?"

"Because I feel the same way. . . ."

THE CHRISTMAS CARROLLS

Barbara Metzger

FAWCETT CREST • NEW YORK

A Fawcett Crest Book
Published by Ballantine Books
Copyright © 1997 by Barbara Metzger

All rights reserved under International and Pan-American Copyright Conventions. Published in the United States by Ballantine Books, a division of Random House, Inc., New York, and simultaneously in Canada by Random House of Canada Limited, Toronto.

http://www.randomhouse.com

Library of Congress Catalog Card Number: 97-90319

ISBN 0-449-22510-0

Manufactured in the United States of America

First Edition: November 1997

10 9 8 7 6 5 4 3 2 1

To my own support group, Louisa D'Alessandro,
my personal play group, Jane Liebell,
and my private writers' guild, Julie Ellis

Prologue

ℒord Carroll considered himself the most fortunate of men. Not only did the earl have his prosperous estate at Winterpark, his health, and his fortune, but he had the love of his dearest friend, his wife, Bess. In addition, he was thrice blessed with the three most perfect daughters ever to grace the countryside. Nay, the entire country.

First came Joia, the eldest, the most beautiful, the earl's favorite. Tall and willowy, blond and blue-eyed, fair Joia was the image of her mother at that age and had his beloved Bess's poise and charm of manner. She brought peace to a man's soul.

Hollice, Bradford Carroll's middle daughter, was the brightest. Stunningly dark-haired, clever Holly was his chess partner, his political debate partner, definitely his favorite. She brought sweet reason to tumultuous times.

Youngest was Meredyth, who tried to be the son the earl didn't have. She was always at his side, hunting, fishing, riding about the estate with him. She even had the red hair and freckles of his own youth. Winsome Merry was absolutely his favorite. She made him smile.

How fortunate he was, the earl thought again as he gazed around the drawing room at his cherished family. Two blond heads were bent over a bit of fabric as Bess and Joia worked on a new altar cloth for the chapel. Holly was at the pianoforte, trying some new composition her doting father was certain she'd soon master. And Merry was sitting on the floor, attempting to teach some manners to the stupidest, ugliest dog she'd ever dragged home from who-knew-where.

Lord Carroll's only regret, besides Merry's latest foundling, was that he hadn't married early enough in life to be around to enjoy his children longer, and perhaps his grandchildren, too. There was no denying that he was getting old, staring at sixty. Of course, if he'd married in his youth, the earl thought, his dearest Bess would have been in her cradle still. He'd never have had the past twenty-one years of her affection, nor the three daughters she'd blessed him with, with all their ruffles and dimples and giggles.

And all their moods and megrims. Three daughters, what a curse! Now he had three young women to find husbands for, three young ladies he'd have to hand over to some brass-faced, callow youths who wouldn't recognize them for the treasures they were. Well, no basket-scramblers were going to get near his little princesses, Lord Carroll swore. No fortune hunters, gamblers, or womanizers, not after he'd suffered through the weeping and wheedling and adolescent willfulness. If there were three gentlemen worthy of his darlings, the earl vowed, he'd find them if he had to comb all the corners of the Empire. No, on second thought, Bradford Carroll would sift through Berkshire, near Winterpark. No here-and-thereian was going to scoop one of his darlings off to the hinterlands where her parents couldn't see her. Bess would be heartbroken.

Ah, Bess! What would she do when he was gone? She'd still be a handsome young woman, with as much wealth as an entailed estate permitted the earl to leave her. She'd have the dower house, of course, but no one to look after her or the vast Carroll family holdings. No one, that was, but his cousin's son, Oliver, his heir, the twit. Why, any one of the earl's daughters would make a better heir to the earldom. Merry knew every tenant and all their troubles; Holly could manage the finances to a farthing; Joia was quietly competent to undertake any task.

2

But they were girls. They could not succeed him, only Oliver could.

And Oliver was a twiddlepoop. Damn and blast! But the earl had a plan. . . .

PART ONE

Comfort and Joia

Chapter One

"*I* won't have it, Bess," Lord Carroll roared, pounding on his cherry-wood desk. "Do you hear me? I won't have it, I say!"

Lady Carroll looked up from the household accounts on her facing cherry-wood escritoire. "I daresay half the county can hear you, my dear, with the windows open. What is it that has you so wrought this morning? You know Dr. Petkin said that agitating your choleric humors can only aggravate the gout."

"The devil take Petkin and his pettifogging quackery," the earl shouted without lowering his voice one jot. He had to make certain the servants clearing away the dishes in the nearby morning room could hear every word, in case his daughters had already finished breaking their fast there. In a houseful of women, whispers stayed secret for perhaps an hour; Lord Carroll saw no reason to waste that much time. He pounded the desk again, in case some stray footman in the hall wasn't paying attention. "I won't have your daughter dragging her feet through another London Season, that's what."

Elizabeth, Lady Carroll, smiled at her husband's theatrics. He'd sooner part with his right arm than with one of his girls, and everyone in the household knew that, from the bootboy to Bartholemew, the butler. "And which of *my* daughters might that be, my dear?"

"The eldest, of course. Merry's not even Out, and Holly's

7

only been up to Town a time or two. Joia is twenty, Bess. She'll be an old maid soon."

"Nonsense, she was last Season's Incomparable."

"And the Season before that, and the one before that, confound it. You know how I hate those boring tonnish affairs, to say nothing of the expense. And I should be here at Winterpark, overseeing those new cottages we're putting in. Besides, we can't get the next chit properly settled till the eldest is wed. Deuce take it, I want to see my grandchildren!"

"Then perhaps you shouldn't glower at all those young men who come calling on Joia whenever we're in Town."

"What, those unlicked cubs licking their lips over her dowry?"

"Not all of them were fortune hunters, dear. Some were from the finest families. I believe you turned away a duke, two barons, and an Austrian prince last spring."

"The duke couldn't sit a horse, one of those lordlings couldn't get his eyes above her collarbone, and the other's eyes popped half out of his head. Do you think I want my grandchildren to look like pug dogs? Or to live in some foreign country?" He pounded the desk again. "Besides, Joia told me to refuse their suits, every one of them and scores more, to say nothing of the unmannered louts who approached her without asking my permission. By Zeus, the chit is too fussy by half. I am putting a stop to all this shilly-shallying and traipsing around the country, Bess. If I never see the inside of Almack's again, it's too soon. The Marriage Mart, hah! The deuced place hasn't accomplished a blasted thing that I can see except force me into knee smalls every Wednesday night. No, this year we'll have a hunt ball instead."

"We have a hunt ball every autumn, Bradford, and a Christmas ball every December, and—"

"Yes, yes, but this year'll be different. We'll invite every eligible *parti* we can think of, every noble sprig and nabob's sprout. And we'll keep them here for an extended house party. We'll get up extra hunts, impromptu dances, even run a steeplechase. Give the gal time to get acquainted, then have her engagement announced at the Christmas party."

The countess raised one golden eyebrow. "And if Joia doesn't care for any of the gentlemen?"

"Either she selects a bridegroom, madam, or I'll choose one for her, see if I don't. She'll be betrothed by the New Year, one way or t'other."

"Now, here's a new start. Would you ask your daughter to marry a man she does not love?"

"I . . . I would dash well demand she fall in love with the man I select!"

Lady Carroll merely shook her head and went back to her accounts. "Yes, dear. Joia has always been a dutiful daughter. I am sure she will try her best."

"She'd better," the earl grumbled. "For I mean to see my girls settled before I stick my spoon in the wall. All of my girls."

Joia wanted to marry, truly she did. She wanted a husband and a home of her own. She wanted children. But not without love, never without love. Unfortunately, Joia hadn't met any gentleman she could love since she was sixteen, when she'd been too shy to speak to the object of her adoration, thank goodness. Lord Kirkendale was now stout, sweaty, and snuff-stained. He was seen at all the London dos while his wife was in the country breeding. Joia was no longer shy, and no longer quick to become infatuated. Sometimes she wondered if she would ever meet a man as good as Papa, whom she'd love with all her heart, as Mama did. That was what she wanted, Joia told herself, what her parents shared. How could Papa expect her to settle for anything less?

No matter how loudly he complained of having to do the pretty in London, Joia knew, her father would never affiance her to someone awful. The idea of sharing her life with a stranger she couldn't care for, though, was awful enough. How dare Papa suggest she make a marriage of convenience, and his convenience at that? Joia wasn't having any of it, nor of his underhanded scheme to plague her with every rake and rattle in Britain.

The way Joia and her sisters had it figured after one week

of the house party, the second sons, the chinless clerics, and the horse-mad half-wits were only invited to Winterpark as window dressing. Joia wasn't about to fall top over trees for any mincing fop, knight of the baize table, or suicidal sportsman, and Papa wouldn't let her wed one even if she did. Well, he might, they all agreed, since Papa could be talked round anything, but he'd be sorely disappointed. So would Joia.

No, the Carroll daughters decided, Papa had not-so-subtly invited the ragtag lot so that his true choices for son-in-law would stand out.

"Papa means you to have Cousin Oliver," Holly stated while the sisters were arranging place cards for that night's formal dinner.

"Papa hates Oliver," Joia reminded her sister. "He gets all red in the face just thinking of the nodcock stepping into his shoes."

"Oliver wouldn't want Papa's shoes," Merry said with a laugh, "for they don't have silver buckles and red heels. In fact, they are more likely to have dirt on their soles, which would send poor Oliver crying for his valet."

Holly smiled at their cousin's dandified manners. "But Papa's shoes are paid for," she insisted. "Oliver would jump at the chance to get his hands on Joia's dowry, and Papa would have to increase his allowance, too. As for Papa, he'd be pleased to see Winterpark stay in the family, with Joia wed to his cousin's son. At least his own grandson would eventually inherit the title and all. And he wouldn't worry so much with you here to curb the rattlepate's excesses."

Joia shuddered. She hadn't envisioned becoming a nanny, only a wife.

"*I* think Papa means you to have Comte Dubournet, Joia. He's titled, wealthy, and *trés charmant*."

"He's a Frenchman, silly, they are all charming. I swear they must be born knowing how to flirt. But you heard Papa, Merry. He'd never want me to go off to France, even if the war ends."

"Yes, but rumor has it that Comte Dubournet is looking to purchase Rendell Hall, almost on our doorstep."

Joia turned to her middle sister. "Is it true, Holly? Is Mr. Rendell selling the Hall?"

"How should I know? I haven't seen the man above twice, for all he's one of our closest neighbors. And I doubt even Evan knows, he sees his father so rarely. Perhaps he'll have more information when he gets here."

"It's not as though Mr. Rendell would be cutting Evan out of his inheritance if he sells to the comte," Merry persisted. "The Hall is not entailed, and neither of them ever lives there. Besides, Evan will inherit Blakely Manor from his mother's father. That's where he was raised, after all, where he calls home."

"But Mr. Rendell can't need the money from the sale of the Hall. Evan's father is said to be one of the warmest men in England."

"He's never in England, though," Merry argued. "No one lives there except the caretakers. If the comte purchases the place, you'd be almost next door. That would please Papa."

"But would it please you, Holly?" Joia asked her middle sister. "Wouldn't you and Evan rather have Rendell Hall than live with Squire and Mrs. Blakely?"

Holly dropped the card she was holding. "Evan Rendell and I have been friends forever. We all have, as you very well know."

"But I thought the wind sat in that quarter," Joia said, trying to wrest the fallen place card out of the mouth of Merry's dog.

"That wind blows only through Papa's cockloft." Still, Holly quickly changed the subject. "What about the viscount, then, Joia? Do you think Papa means you to have him?"

"What, Lord Comfort? Papa could never suppose I'd accept that rake."

"But he is devilishly handsome."

"And well he knows it! The man is self-important and supercilious!"

"He's the Duke of Carlisle's heir, though. You know that must count for something with Papa," Holly reasoned.

"It counts for naught with me, since the man is a confirmed rake. His name has been linked to every ballet dancer and—" She paused at Holly's cough and nod in their younger sister's wide-eyed direction. "That is, Papa cannot approve of Craighton Ellingsworth, no matter whose heir he is."

"Then you might as well pair him with Aubergine Willenborg." Merry held out the dashing young widow's name card, proving she wasn't quite as innocent as her sisters wished to pretend. Mrs. Willenborg was a connection of Mama's who had been invited to round out the numbers, as well as she rounded out her low-cut gowns.

"Perfect!" Joia exclaimed. "That should keep the viscount contented, and out of contention for Papa's little game."

"Ahem." All eyes turned to where the butler was straightening the silverware at the other end of the long table. Mr. Bartholemew had been the family's butler since before there was a family. He might be slower answering the front door, but his hearing was as acute as ever.

"Yes, Barty? Are you in Papa's confidence?"

The old butler sighed in regret for lost opportunities. M'lord was playing this hand close to his chest. "No, m'ladies. I simply wished to inform you that the household staff favors Master Oliver's chances at odds of two to one, while Jake reports the stable crew appears to be leaning toward *monsieur le comte*."

Joia wasn't the least surprised that her affairs were public knowledge. "Where are you placing your bets, Barty?"

The butler *ahem*ed again in indignation. Wager on the family? Before all the cards were dealt? "I believe Master Evan is bringing some young officers and old schoolmates when he arrives for the hunt. His invitation did include any of his friends who might be interested. Perhaps one of those young men will suit."

"What about the viscount?" Joia wanted to know.

Bartholemew polished a speck off one of the forks. "Lord Comfort has spent the two days since his arrival visiting various horse breeders. He is not widely perceived as, ah, ready to establish his nursery."

Which meant, Joia knew, that Viscount Comfort was still finding comfort in the arms of every willing widow across the width of England. Joia mightn't be as smart as Holly or as spirited as Merry, but she was no porcelain doll to be moved from shelf to shelf at anyone's whim. Bradford Carroll, Earl of Carroll, hadn't bred any spineless fools. Joia was worldly wise enough to realize that, standing heir to a dukedom, Comfort must be under more pressure than she to marry and ensure the succession. Furthermore, his father, the duke, was one of Papa's closest friends. The viscount had wealth, breeding, looks—and the morals of a maggot. Joia wasn't having any of him, no matter Papa's machinations. She had money of her own and, being the daughter of an earl, had a title of her own. Lady Joia Carroll would rather stay an old maid than wed a wandering-eyed womanizer. So there.

Chapter Two

There he was, holding himself above the company at afternoon tea. Lord Comfort hadn't kept his distance from Aubergine Willenborg at dinner last night, Joia and her sisters had gleefully noted. Why, a crumb could hardly have fallen between the two. At alternate courses the viscount had flirted with his other dinner partner, having Mama laughing and blushing like a girl. Mama! Good grief, did the rake have no conscience?

After dinner the company had gotten up card games. The viscount was claimed as partner by Mrs. Squire Blakely, yet another susceptible female, so Aubergine had draped herself around the French nobleman. Joia was still doing her duty by the vicar and his wife when Comfort retired. This morning she'd discovered her quarry already out of the house by breakfast. The viscount was studying her father's stud books in the stable office, according to Merry, who'd had it from Jake, their head groom. Joia was determined to speak to the libertine before one more day passed, before he had one more conversation with Papa. She could just imagine whose breeding lines they were discussing.

Joia poured out a cup of tea, adding enough sugar to gag one of the brood mares, then made her way toward the windows where his lordship now stood in solitary splendor. He was a magnificent creature, Joia conceded. Tall, dark, and handsome—de rigueur for rakes—the self-assured peer left all the other young men in the room looking like country rustics or caper merchants. The viscount's understated elegance made Cousin Oliver's yellow Cossack trousers and spotted neckcloth look like something found at Astley's Circus. Then again, Cousin Oliver would need half the sawdust on Astley's floor in order to fill out the viscount's wide-shouldered bottle green coat or form-fitting buckskin breeches. So it wasn't just his wealth and title that made Lord Comfort such a successful rake, Joia acknowledged with a mental shrug that couldn't spill the tea. He was still a rake.

To be fair, Comfort didn't prey on young girls. He never attended debutante balls and such, so their paths had seldom crossed, but she'd never heard his name mentioned in the same breath as that of a wellborn female of marriageable age. Which was how it was going to remain, if Lady Joia had anything to say about it.

When she reached his side, she had plenty to say: "Tea, my lord? I added sugar. I'm sorry I haven't had a chance to properly welcome you to Winterpark. Oh, and I wouldn't marry you if you were the last man on earth."

Whether it was the sugar, the shock, or the slight pat Joia gave to the viscount's sleeve as he raised the cup to his lips, Lord Comfort's tea landed on Lord Comfort's shirtfront, waistcoat, and cravat. And Lady Carroll's Aubusson carpet. "Oh, dear," Joia said as his lordship hastily excused himself. "The poor carpet."

Joia hummed to herself as she dressed for dinner that evening. A weight was off her shoulders. Now she could begin to enjoy the house party. Perhaps one of the young men would grow conversable upon closer acquaintance. Perhaps one would grow a beard to hide his weak chin. Who knew? Perhaps tonight she would fall in love at last.

Joia put on her favorite bishop's blue gown, the one whose neckline was the lowest Papa would allow. Her hair was gathered atop her head in a matching blue ribbon except for one long gold curl falling over her nearly bare shoulder. For an old maid, she'd do. Happily she tripped down the stairs to the parlor where the company was gathering for sherry before dinner. Unhappily, the first person she saw was the viscount, who gave her a dark look before turning to Aubergine, at his side like a sticking plaster. The widow was batting her lashes—blackened with kohl, Joia was certain—so hard that the viscount's intricately folded neckcloth was fluttering. Joia also noticed that the bodice of Mrs. Willenborg's gown had less fabric than the blue ribbon in her own hair. She smiled. His lordship wouldn't miss his opera dancers too badly before taking himself back to Town.

Meanwhile Joia intended to enjoy herself, accepting the flattering attentions of Comte Dubournet. Somehow the usual compliments sounded less banal in French, if less sincere. Even Cousin Oliver, in his puce waistcoat and lemon-striped pantaloons, managed to say something not too offensive: "I say, Cuz, that gown is still becoming. And that curl's a nice touch, even if short locks are all the crack."

Then, long before Bartholemew could be expected to announce dinner, the viscount was bowing in front of her. "Perhaps you would be kind enough to tell me something of the history of the tapestry on the far wall?"

There was nothing for Joia to do but smile and accept the arm Lord Comfort was holding out for her. She walked with him across the length of the room, gritting her teeth at the knowing smiles on all the faces they passed.

"Miss Carroll, is it?" the viscount asked as though he didn't know.

"You are correct that I am the eldest daughter of the house, my lord, but I am Lady Joia."

"Ah, yes. I wasn't entirely sure about the lady part."

Joia was certain the lout was referring to the incident over tea, not the proper form of address. She turned from him toward the wall hanging, but not before noticing, begrudgingly, how attractive he looked in the black and white evening wear. Joia started to describe the tapestry, a depiction of the first Lord Carroll, or Karol, or Carl, fighting his liege's battles to win the earldom. She was dutifully explaining how the symbolism of the dragons was repeated on the family's coat of arms when Lord Comfort gestured for a footman. He lifted two glasses off the tray, then waited for the fellow to get out of earshot.

"Lady Joia," the viscount said in a measured tone, "I am sure you know more about tapestries than I could care about, but I brought you here because I have three things to say to you. One, I believe a *lady* waits to refuse an offer of marriage until after she receives one. Two, I am not in the market for a wife. And three, if I were, I would never choose some spoiled, flawed Diamond with all the warmth of a rock."

With that, he handed over the second glass of sherry. Somehow the glass slipped and the sticky red stuff dripped down Joia's décolletage. "You did that on purpose," she sputtered as the viscount reached for his handkerchief.

"What, discommode a lady? I assure you, a gentleman never would." Comfort held out the lace-edged cloth toward where the sherry was staining the bodice of her gown. "Shall I?"

Joia was late for dinner, of course. She had to enter when everyone was enjoying the second course, forcing her supper partners to rise while she was seated. She made hasty apologies like the veriest peagoose, avoiding her mother's eyes.

She couldn't avoid her mother for long, however. As soon as the ladies left the gentlemen to their port, Lady Carroll beckoned her eldest daughter to her side in the Chinese Room.

"Two mishaps in one day?" Lady Carroll's eyebrows rose. "Now, if it were Hollice, I might understand. With her nose in a book, or without her spectacles, she does tend to be awkward. And Meredyth, unfortunately, still exhibits a tendency toward girlish exuberance. But you, my dear?"

"I am sorry, Mama. It's just that the viscount . . ."

"Yes, I can see where such a paragon could turn a girl's head, dearest, but I thought you above such nonsense."

"Turn my head? It's no such thing, Mama. He infuriates me, the cad, the coxcomb, the conceited—"

"Guest in our home."

"Yes, Mama." Joia turned to engage old Lady Matthews in

conversation, feeling like a chastened schoolgirl, Comfort be hanged.

The next morning Joia followed her father to the estate office directly after breakfast.

"I won't marry him, Papa, and that's final."

"And just who won't you be marrying this week, my dear?" he teased.

"Your pet peer, and well you know it!"

"What, did Comfort offer? I did see you go off with him before dinner."

"No, Papa, he did not offer. But that's why he's here, isn't it? So you and the Duke of Carlisle can continue your lines."

"Well, yes, actually, but with our Thoroughbreds, not our children. We've been meaning to mix the bloodlines this age, but never got around to it. Now Comfort came into a bit of land of his own in Ireland and intends to set up a new stud. He's here to select some mares for breeding."

"That's all?" Joia asked, beginning to feel a complete gudgeon.

Lord Carroll shrugged. "What else? Oh, you thought he might be in the Marriage Market? I'm sorry, puss, you'll have to look elsewhere." He held a hand up at her protests. "Don't mean you ain't perfect, my favorite daughter and all."

"Papa, you tell that to all of us."

"And it's true every time, I swear."

"Papa!"

"Yes, well, I don't mean Comfort is above your touch, either. It's just that he ain't interested in innocents. You'd have to dance naked on the table to catch his eye, puss. Of course, I'd have to send you to your aunt Irmentrude in Wales if you did such a thing, but you get my drift. Leave the viscount to knowing 'uns like Aubergine Willenborg. She understands how to play the game."

"Marriage isn't a game."

"You see, that's my point." The earl shook his head, almost in sorrow. "No, I doubt you could bring that young man up to scratch no matter how hard you tried."

"Fine. Good," Joia declared on her way out the door, vowing to do that very thing. Oh, she'd never marry his libertine lordship, but she'd show him that proper young ladies had passion too, even if she had to flirt with the émigré comte and Cousin Oliver to prove it. Flawed Diamond, hah!

Next to scratch on Lord Carroll's door was, not unexpectedly, the viscount, dressed for riding.

"Come in, my boy, come in. What, have you a question about one of the horses?"

Comfort didn't take the seat his host offered, choosing instead to pace in front of the earl's desk. "No, sir. My question concerns the purpose of my visit."

"What, not finding any of the cattle to your liking?"

"I like the horses very well, my lord. Your stables are some of the finest in the land. I am concerned, however, that you and my father had some other matchmaking scheme in mind beyond the mares and stallions, when you invited me here and he urged me to accept."

"What, you think we're trying to legshackle you to one of my daughters? I saw you with Joia last evening. Beautiful gal, eh?"

"One of the finest in the land." Comfort echoed his previous compliment, noting that the earl hadn't denied the charge.

"She's a beauty, all right, just like her mother." Lord Carroll beamed, then frowned. "Too bad she's the most finicky female I've ever known. I can't tell you the number of likely lads I've had to turn away. Don't have daughters, my boy, they'll give you gray hair." He patted his own silvered mane, then laughed. "When you're ready, of course."

"I'll remember your advice, my lord, when I am ready." Comfort waited.

"About that other matter, you don't have to worry. No offense, my boy, but Joia wouldn't have a man of your stamp."

So the chit thought she was too good for him? Comfort tapped his riding crop against his boot.

The earl tried to explain. "That is, I'd be proud to welcome you to the family, lad, if you were so inclined, but Joia's been properly raised. Too sheltered, perhaps. She'll make some man a loyal, loving wife, but not until she finds one she can trust, if you take my meaning."

"She doubts my honor?" Comfort asked disbelievingly. Gentlemen were known to meet at dawn over lesser slurs.

"It's not a question of your honor, my boy. Gentleman and all. It's fidelity that has my girl in a swivet. She doesn't want one of those modern marriages where husband and wife go their own way after the heir is born, if not before. I cannot say that I'd look with favor on such a match for one of my lasses. So no, my boy, you don't have to worry about finding me holding a pistol to your head if you walk out in the spinney with Joia. I'd never force you into marriage, not when it would make one of my girls miserable for the rest of her life."

So Lady Joia believed he would not be faithful to his wife when he took one. Of course he would, Comfort fumed. He wasn't about to give his vows, else, which was why he wasn't yet wed despite his father's urgings, cajolery, and outright threats. He hadn't found a woman who could hold his interest. Lady Joia certainly couldn't. And he wasn't good enough for her? Hah! Miss Prunes and Prisms had a lesson or two to learn about men in the meantime, fiend take the plaguey chit, and Comfort was just the man to teach her.

After the viscount stormed out of the office, jaw clenched, knuckles white around the riding stick, Lord Carroll checked his pocket watch and smiled in satisfaction. He'd already done a fine day's work and it wasn't even nine o'clock in the morning.

Chapter Three

*J*oia knew she couldn't become a dasher overnight, but she could dashed well show a certain cocksure clunch that she wasn't any milk-and-water miss. A judicious snip of her scissors here, a dab from the rouge pot there. That was all it took, she was sure, less lace, more skin. Joia even let her maid trim some of her long hair so tiny tendrils curled around her cheeks, as though a lover's hand had freed the blond tresses from their pins.

"You look like you just got out of bed," Merry said.

But Holly sagely nodded her approval. "That's the point, silly."

And Joia flirted more, too. Didn't all sophisticated ladies? She wasn't as brazen as the Widow Willenborg—she'd have been sent to Aunt Irmentrude on the instant—but she did manage to keep one spotted youth perpetually ablush, and she inspired another to sudden versification. She let the Frenchman—Phillipe, he insisted—hold her so close during a waltz that the Almack's patronesses would have rescinded her vouchers, and she even feigned interest in Cousin Oliver's lisping catalog of his snuffboxes, for Papa's sake.

Lord Carroll harrumphed a few times at the lower necklines, but Lady Carroll frowned, especially after Joia complimented Cousin Oliver on his new peacock-embroidered waistcoat. "Are you sure you aren't sickening for something, my dear? You haven't been yourself at all these few days."

No, but she'd been a woman of the world, and she'd made sure the high-nosed Nonesuch saw it whenever he left the paddocks and stables and Mrs. Willenborg's side. "La, you shouldn't say such naughty things, my—Phillipe," she cooed for Lord Comfort's benefit, not pulling her hand out of the Frenchman's grasp until the viscount turned away.

Soon enough, Joia's efforts began to bear fruit. Lemons.

She'd agreed to go for a ride with Cousin Oliver, for Papa's sake. Oliver didn't hunt because his clothes might get mud-spattered. He didn't race because his hair would get all wind-blown—or his hairpiece might blow away. He didn't drive because Papa wouldn't let his ham-fisted heir near his high-bred cattle. And Oliver didn't take walks lest he scuff his new boots, which were likely not paid for yet, so Joia consented to what Oliver considered an agreeable ramble through the countryside: an agonizingly slow perambulation atop the oldest horses in Papa's stable. After trying to coax him into a gallop—Oliver, not her ancient mount—Joia concluded that the next Earl of Carroll was a craven. The pockets-to-let peer-to-be was petrified of horses! No wonder Papa was so affronted by the thought of this fribble taking over Winterpark and its marvelous stables.

Once they were past the home woods and the outbuildings, Oliver did allow as how it might be pleasant to have a bit of a trot, if his cousin was sure there were no rabbit holes. "Wouldn't want to jeopardize a lady, don't you know."

Not two minutes later, Joia felt old Nelson come up lame. She pulled him to a halt and dismounted, without waiting for Oliver's assistance. "Nelson can't be ridden," she told her cousin after examining the hoof, while Oliver stayed mounted. Joia looked around for her groom so they could switch saddles and Tom could walk Nelson back. The dratted fellow was nowhere in sight. They couldn't have outdistanced him, Joia knew, not at the pace they'd been keeping, so Tom must have had a problem with his own horse. He should have let her know, Joia thought, but she was more concerned over the old horse than her missing groom. "We'll just have to walk home," she said, waiting for Oliver to offer her his mount. They didn't *both* have to walk.

"Neither of us has to walk, Cuz. We can ride double on my horse."

She didn't bother looking at him, just gathered her skirts over her arm so they wouldn't tangle as she led Nelson back the way they had come. "That would be highly improper, Oliver. It's bad enough that we are out here alone, out of sight."

"It wouldn't be improper if we were betrothed."

"What?" Now she did look at him, aghast. "Betrothed?"

He'd finally dismounted, awkwardly enough, and came to take Nelson's reins, Joia thought. Instead he grabbed for her own hand and squeezed it. "I've come to see that you cared for me. I hadn't thought we'd rub along so well together until you proved so attentive to my interests. Why, you positively drooled over my snuffboxes, didn't you? And you know this is what your father has always had in mind."

Joia tried to free her hand, but he held tight. Her skirts were trailing in the dirt again. Obviously she wasn't going to reclaim her hand until she'd given her cousin some kind of answer. "I am terribly sorry, Oliver, but I never meant to give you the impression that I'd welcome an offer. That is . . ."

"Nonsense, Cuz. No one's watching, so you don't have to pretend to this false modesty. I know you're interested in me, my pet, so don't play coy now. I've seen the way you smile at me. I know what you want."

Then he pulled her closer and pressed his limp, wet lips against hers. No, Joia thought, this was not what she wanted. She couldn't do this, not even for Papa. So she kicked Oliver in the shin with her thick-soled riding boot until he released her, cursing. "There," she told him, "now you're as lame as your offer. You're as lame as old Nelson, but he's better company."

She led the horse off toward home, not even caring about her skirts anymore, she was that angry. She was outraged with Oliver, of course, and furious that she'd brought his repulsive advances down on herself. Mostly, though, she was angry with Lord Comfort, who was responsible for the entire hobble. She was too busy muttering to Nelson about the male species in general, present company excluded, of course, to hear Oliver ride alongside her.

"Come on, Cuz, you cannot walk back by yourself. Uncle will have my hide. Leave the beast and ride behind me. He'll find his own way home."

Leave a horse loose? Papa would have *her* hide! That was how little Oliver knew of Papa, or horses, or women. He proved it by continuing: "I'm sure that with a bit of reflection, you'll see the benefits of my offer. The future of the stables, security for your mother, the continuance of the Carroll line, don't you know. I don't doubt you were merely overwhelmed by my offer. I'm prepared to forgive your childish temper tantrum and accept your apology."

"Overwhelmed? Apology? I'll show you my apology, you mincing mawworm!" Joia brought her riding crop down on the broad rump of Oliver's mount, sending the animal into the first gallop the gelding had had in years, with Oliver screeching and hanging on for dear life. "I'll apologize to the horse tomorrow."

Joia expected to meet her groom coming to find her, especially if Oliver made it back to the stables. Then again, his horse had been facing in the opposite direction. She didn't expect to meet Comte Dubournet strolling up the carriageway, nor was she pleased with his company at this moment. The count didn't ask if there had been an accident, if she was hurt, if he should run for help, if she needed assistance with the horse. Instead he wanted to pay her pretty compliments.

"*Enchanté, ma belle.* As beautiful as ever."

She was all over damp, her riding habit was in a shambles, and her feet hurt. The man must need spectacles. That or his attics were to let.

He noticed her frown. "To a man in love, his inamorata is always beautiful."

In love? "Excuse me, my lord, I really must get poor Nelson back to the stables."

"Phillipe, *chérie.* But no, you mustn't rush off, now that I have you alone. It's why *Pére* Carroll invited me, no?"

Joia added her father to the list of malfeasant males. "No,

24

that is, I have no idea why he invited you, but I'm sure it wasn't so we could be alone."

"*Mais oui, chérie.* How else am I to lay my heart at your feet, to pledge eternal devotion? With all your encouragement, I knew I didn't have to wait before declaring myself."

"But I never meant to—"

Joia never meant to let him kiss her, either, but he did that too, grabbing her shoulders and crushing her lips with his. At least his kiss wasn't all slobbery like Oliver's. If she just waited a moment, he'd be done so she could thank him for the honor and be on her way. One one-thousand, two one-thousand, she counted. Instead, the madman tried to stick his tongue in her mouth! Ugh.

Papa'd always said that if she was angry enough to slap a man, she might as well make it count, so Joia pushed Dubournet away, balled up her fist, and hit him square in the nose.

Now she had spatters of blood on her habit and the broken feather from her hat drooping down her forehead, but she was that much closer to home and a hot bath. All she had to do was get Nelson to his stall—with a word to the head stableman about her missing groom—then creep into the house by the back door.

Lord Comfort was in the stable office, copying out some pedigrees he wanted to study. He'd seen Lady Joia ride out with her clodpole of a cousin, then he'd heard the groom come back, saying he'd been dismissed. The viscount went back to his records. The willful chit was Carroll's problem, not his. Still, his eyes couldn't help straying to the rear window as he waited for her return. When he finally caught a glimpse of her, alone, leading her horse, he almost jumped up to sound the alarm, but the Frenchman was already there.

Dubournet appeared to have matters—and the minx—well in hand. Comfort turned away in disgust. Little Miss Morality was no better than she ought to be, the hypocrite. Then, out of the corner of his eye, he thought he saw her struggle. In a flash Lord Comfort was out the rear office door, tearing down the path, in time to see Carroll's Incomparable land the Frenchman a facer that would have done Gentleman Jackson proud.

The viscount spared hardly a glance for the fallen count, merely tossing him a handkerchief to stem the flow of claret. "Are you all right, Lady Joia? Shall I send for a carriage?" Meanwhile he ran knowing hands down Nelson's foreleg.

Joia was so enraged she was surprised that blasted feather wasn't smoldering on her forehead. Why did it have to be Comfort to see her in such an unfavorable light? She snatched the hat off her head and threw it to the ground. "No, I am not all right! I have been insulted and abused and—"

"And I bet your hand hurts like the devil. You should put it on ice as soon as you reach your room." Comfort was trying to fend off the tears he could hear behind her anger. Those magnificent blue eyes might be flashing fire now, but they'd soon be red and weepy if he knew anything about women. He took up Nelson's reins and placed his other hand under her elbow to lead her on. "By-the-by, that was a flush hit. My compliments on your science."

"I did manage to draw his cork for him, didn't I?" Joia said with a chuckle, earning her a high mark for courage in Comfort's book. The beauty had bottom, at least, to make up for her total brainlessness, going off alone and unprotected. He thought all debutantes, especially gorgeous heiresses, were taught better than that.

"Should I be sending a cart out for Master Oliver, also?" he asked, bringing a touch of embarrassed color to her pale cheeks.

"Only if he doesn't return by nightfall, the gudgeon."

"Not such a gudgeon for trying to secure his future, assuming that's what he did, of course."

"What, you don't censure him for making unwanted advances?"

"How was he to know they were unwanted, after you'd led the poor fool on? Yes, and Dubournet, too. What did you expect when you rode off without a groom? You practically issued an invitation."

Joia gasped. "I never!"

Now Comfort was angry, and he didn't want to ask himself why. "What, back to Miss Prim and Proper? You were playing the tease, and well you know it. You set out to fire up their blood, then got in a snit when you smelled smoke."

"How dare you!"

"It's only the truth." Lord Comfort knew because his own senses had been stirred by her flirtatious glances, her swaying hips and daring necklines. Hell, she looked so adorably disheveled this very moment that he could barely resist taking liberties himself. Then she stumbled—her boots were not made for walking—and he immediately put his arm around her, which was a grave challenge to his self-discipline. "And I dare the same way those other unfortunate fools dared."

Comfort's kiss wasn't like Oliver's sloppy mauling or the Frenchman's assault. It wasn't like any of the stolen kisses she'd suffered over the years, perhaps because this one was not so much stolen from her as given to her. The viscount's lips were warm and soft, tingly and hard, all at once. Joia's feet didn't hurt anymore because she couldn't feel them, only a delicious spreading glow. This kiss was all she'd ever dreamed one should be—and it meant absolutely nothing to a practiced rake like Comfort.

Joia stepped back. The viscount released her immediately, with a quizzical look on his handsome face. This time Joia defended herself the way Papa had taught her to do if she was in extreme danger. Oh, she was.

"Well, puss," Lord Carroll told her when Joia was through complaining about his guests and his grooms, "seems to me you went about the whole thing wrong. Not that you need to fret about it happening again, for it won't, by George." Two broken pencils already lay scattered on the desk in front of the irate earl. "But the fact is, if you were trying to bring Comfort up to scratch, you were far off the mark. I told you, I doubt he'll step into parson's mousetrap till he's ready to set up his nursery. By all accounts, you put paid to that notion."

Chapter Four

$\mathcal{L}$ord Carroll decided the gentlemen should all go target shooting the next morning. "The ladies are starting to decorate for the hunt ball, so we'll do better out of the house. You, too, Oliver. Fresh air might just improve that pasty complexion of yours."

Oliver grew paler yet under the face paint that was hiding miscellaneous cuts and bruises, some from the horse's neck bones where he'd been clinging, some from the ground when he hadn't clung hard enough, and one from a certain gentleman's fist. At least his nose wasn't a huge purple beet between his eyes like the Frenchman's, who was also claiming a riding mishap. "We're not going riding, are we?"

"No, things are at sixes and sevens at the stables right now. Shorthanded, don't you know. In fact, we'll have to carry the targets and the guns ourselves. Come along now."

When they reached the designated shooting area and the wooden frames had been covered with paper targets, Oliver found himself matched for the competition with the three men he was least wishing to address: Dubournet, Comfort, and his cousin Carroll. The earl apologized again for making them all work so hard at their own entertainment. "Had to let some of the grooms go, don't you know." He shook his silver-haired head. "I say that if you can't count on a chap's loyalty, you shouldn't be paying his salary."

The earl was loading his pistol while he spoke, eyeing the

target and the other shooters. "All I asked was that they look after my animals and my family. Dastards didn't do their jobs. Can you imagine a bloke jeopardizing his whole future for a few extra coins?" He took aim at the paper circles. "Of course, I can still protect what's mine."

Bull's-eye.

Oliver's hand was shaking so badly his shot didn't even hit the target. The Frenchman fared slightly better, hitting the outer ring. Only Comfort's shot came close to the earl's, whose turn it was again. This time he hardly studied the distance before firing. "And I can still see what's going on around me."

Bull's-eye.

"See that, lads? I'm not in my dotage yet. Remember it."

Remember? Oliver couldn't remember how to load his pistol. The earl took the gun out of his shaking fingers and spoke softly, for Oliver's ears only. "I have a few more good years, Ollie, so don't go taking out any post-obits on me. Don't go spending my blunt before it's in your pocket, either. If I have anything to say about it, you won't get a farthing. You sure as Hades won't get my daughter."

Bull's-eye.

Joia decided to be herself, instead of a femme fatale. She'd always had enough admirers, without all the unwanted advances. A bit of lace here, a nosegay of flowers there, filled in the necklines. She left the trailing ringlets in her hair, liking the softer look and deciding that dressing to please herself didn't mean she had to look like an antidote. And acting to please herself did not mean she couldn't be polite to her parents' guests or enjoy the preparations for the annual ball. Her decision was made simpler by the count's hasty removal from Winterpark and Oliver's hasty removal from any room she entered. She'd even managed to cry pax with Viscount Comfort after his handsome apology. At least he sounded sincere, unlike Cousin Oliver, who muttered through begging her pardon in order to get back into Papa's good graces, if such a thing was possible.

Comfort was also being more pleasant. He was nearly finished selecting the mares for breeding, he said, so he had more time to be sociable. Joia thought that he was merely favoring the sisters' company in an effort to avoid Aubergine's. The buxom young widow had focused her sights more closely on the viscount, now that her other prey had made good his escape. None of the remaining male guests was as wealthy, wellborn, and unwed as Craighton Ellingsworth, Lord Comfort. Aubergine had done well for herself, rising from barrister's daughter to rich widow. Now she craved the respectability and social acceptance she'd never find as an unfettered female. What was more respectable than the title of duchess, when the viscount succeeded his father? Comfort realized his peril, Joia thought; that's why she and her sisters were suddenly seeing more of him.

To his credit, the viscount didn't appear to mind that Holly consistently beat him at chess, or that Merry's dog ate the tassels off his Hessians. It was Comfort, in fact, who finally named the sorry beast. Downsy, he became, not because his coat was soft—it was more like a boar's bristle than a fowl's fluff—but because "Down, sir" was all anyone ever said to the mongrel. The viscount also kindly volunteered to help Merry practice her dance steps before the ball, to calm her nerves. Merry wasn't quite Out, but she'd been attending local assemblies since last spring. This was the first time she'd be permitted to dance at her parents' hunt ball, with all eyes upon her. Holly played the pianoforte while Joia took the part of the dance instructor, trying to keep her traitorous mind from wondering what it would be like to be held in Lord Comfort's arms.

"Are you certain you won't have him, Joia?" Merry asked later when they were helping the footmen drape the ballroom in gold-colored bunting.

"Him who?"

"Comfort, of course, you noddy. For if you don't want him, I've decided that he'll suit me to a cow's thumb."

"You only like the idea of helping him start that new stud in Ireland," Holly put in.

"Not true. He's a graceful dancer, he's kind to animals, and his eyes are the nicest brown."

With little golden flecks, Joia mentally added, but aloud she said, "That's no way to select a husband, goose. You have to consider his character more. For all his polished manners, Merry, Lord Comfort would only break your heart. He's still a rake."

"But you like him, Joia, you know you do."

"Yes, I suppose I do. I just don't trust him."

The Carroll ladies were to wear complementing colors for the ball, colors that would be echoed in the baskets of fall flowers that would decorate Winterpark. The place might be famous for its holly and yew, its mistletoe-hung oaks, but Lady Carroll's gardens were never more magnificent than in the autumn.

Merry's gown should have been white, befitting her youth, but white only emphasized her freckles, so Lady Carroll relented and permitted a pale yellow. Holly's brown hair and creamy complexion were stunning against the ecru lace of her gown, and Joia's burnt orange proclaimed her a woman, not a pastel-pretty debutante. Their mother would wear burgundy.

The gowns needed a final fitting, so the houseguests were invited to come along to the neighboring village to shop, visit the lending library, tour the local church, and meet up for luncheon at the Carrolton Arms Inn. There were two carriages for the older ladies and Oliver, who announced that he'd keep Cousin Elizabeth and her companions company, lest they feel the lack of male escort. Aubergine also joined them, knowing better than to show her less-than-proficient riding skills when the Carroll sisters were around. Let them arrive all wind-tossed, sun-browned, and exerted; she'd show a certain aristocrat that she knew what was fitting for a real lady. Oliver would have agreed, if Mrs. Willenborg had deigned to engage him in conversation.

The village of Carrolton had enough shops to amuse the ladies, and the inn boasted the finest ale in Berkshire for the gentlemen. As they parted at the livery stable, where the horses and carriages would be left, Lady Carroll directed everyone to meet at the inn in two hours' time. Holly wished to stop at the lending library first, to see if Mr. Reid had received the latest shipment of books from London. Comfort went along with her, hoping to purchase a volume on chess strategy, and a manual on dog training while he was at it. Joia and her youngest sister followed in their mother's wake on the way to Madame Genevieve's—which used to be Jenny's Dress Shop before French modistes became the rage, with raised prices.

When Merry stopped to look in the window of the jewelers, a rough-dressed man stepped up to Joia. "My lady, ma'am, can I beg a minute of your time?" It was Tom, the dismissed groom, with his hat in his hand. "To make apologies, is all."

He looked so contrite, Joia nodded and sent Merry on ahead. "I'll catch up with you in a moment."

"Could we head back toward the livery, miss, please? I can't have Mr. Humphreys thinkin' I ain't doin' my job."

Joia thought he didn't want his new employer to see him asking for his old position back, so she told him, "It's not necessary, Tom, and to be honest, no matter how you beg my pardon, Papa won't have you back at Winterpark."

"No, he were decent enough to tell Humphreys I'm good with horses. I don't 'spect nothin' more, just want to say what needs to be said, my lady, try to explain about me poor sick mum and the money and all."

So Joia followed the groom around the side of the livery barn, out of sight of the villagers and Humphreys, the blacksmith and livery owner. Waiting there was Oliver.

Joia spun on her heel, but Tom was blocking her way back to the main road. "You cur."

Tom just shrugged and jingled some coins in his pocket, so Joia turned back to her cousin. "What is the meaning of this, Oliver? Papa will have your head for sure."

Oliver was standing close, but not close enough to kick. "Just wanted to talk, Cuz, private-like."

"Oh? I could have sworn you were avoiding my company."

"Couldn't talk in front of all the swells or the nursery crowd." He jerked his head toward where Merry was disappearing down the street. " 'Sides, I changed my mind."

"You mean my father's threats changed it for you. Well, nothing has changed *my* mind, sirrah. I don't care how deeply you're in dun territory, I would sooner take a toad to husband than you." She made to leave, misdoubting Tom would dare go so far as to stop her, but Oliver grabbed her arm. For such a fribble, he was still bigger than she, and stronger.

"You haven't heard me out, missy." He pulled her farther down the alley, out of the groom's hearing. "You're right about my punting on tick. A gentleman has certain standards to maintain."

Joia made an unladylike snort. "Gentleman, hah!"

Oliver ignored her. "And I'm afraid your dowry has become necessary to my continued health. Certain, ah, business associates have become fairly insistent about their loans." Especially since Lord Carroll let it be known through the servants' grapevine that he wouldn't make good on his heir's debts.

"What, you've gone to the moneylenders? You're even more of a slowtop than I thought, if that's possible."

"What choice did I have, with your father giving me short shrift?" he asked bitterly, forgetting to lisp.

"He would have helped you find an occupation. He tried to get you to take up one of the borough seats in Parliament."

"What, the Commons? I'm to be earl one day." The current earl couldn't keep that from Oliver, but he could manage to hand him an empty title, empty, that is, of anything Oliver could sell off to pay his mounting debts. The earl could tie the estate up in trusts and torts, if he couldn't find a way to circumvent the succession altogether. Oliver was worried. Besides, who knew how long the old stick could hang on? Oliver had to guarantee his future, and he had to do it now. "When we marry, the money will stay in the family."

"Are you deaf, besides dunder-headed? I shall not marry you, Oliver, never."

"Not even to ensure your mother's well-being?"

"My father sees to Mama's every comfort, you clunch."

"But he's old, Joia. You know that when I inherit I can control her income and circumstances. Why, I can even invite Aunt Irmentrude to come share the dower house with her."

Joia shuddered, but still held firm: "Papa will make sure that my mother is well protected against swine like you."

"Ah, but can he protect her against finding out about his illegitimate son?"

Joia laughed. "Don't be absurd. Papa would never be unfaithful to my mother. You know he adores her."

"My sweet, innocent cousin. I adore my saffron waistcoat. That doesn't mean I want to wear it every day."

"My father is not like you, you swine. And how dare you compare my mother—or any wife, for that matter—to one of your hideous rags?"

Oliver studied the manicure on his right hand. "The boy is eight years old."

Eyes narrowed, Joia asked, "How do you know? What proof do you have?"

Oliver wasn't about to admit he'd been rifling his cousin's desk last year looking for cash when he'd come upon a notebook with odd notations. A bit of digging had uncovered some interesting facts about the irreproachable earl. Oliver wasn't worried about the boy; he was a bastard, after all. He just couldn't figure a way to use the information, until now. "Your father supports him. I saw a caretaker's accounting."

Joia shook her head. "No. It cannot be."

"But it is." Oliver was enjoying himself immensely. The sanctimonious earl and his starched-up daughter were about to be taken down a peg or two. Or three. "Think of your mother. Why, she'd never be able to hold her head up here in Carrolton again, much less London. Think of the scandal—and of your sisters. I doubt if Miss Merry would even be presented. Hoyden that she is, that might be a blessing, except I wouldn't wish to have such a hobbledehoy female on my hands forever. And Holly. I doubt if even the Rendell cub could be convinced to take her, his grandfather Blakely being such a high stickler."

Joia needed to sit down. She needed to cry on her mother's shoulder. "Oh, Mama," she moaned.

"I knew you'd come around to my way of thinking. I expect you to convince your doting father that our betrothal is your fondest desire. I expect it is, now. The announcement can be made at the hunt ball. If not, a letter will arrive on your mother's doorstep, and another one at every London newspaper. I'll leave you to think on it, my heart's Joy. Just don't think for too long. My creditors are quite anxious."

Chapter Five

*S*omeone touched Joia's shoulder. She jumped up from the crate she'd collapsed onto and turned, hands formed into fists. Comfort stepped back, his own hands teasingly raised in surrender. "I swear I have no evil intentions. When you didn't join your sisters I thought I'd just make sure you— Good grief, what happened?"

The viscount had gotten a better look at Joia, her pale face and anguished eyes. He'd seen her go off with one of the ostlers, an odd enough occurrence in itself, then he'd seen Oliver Carroll depart the same alleyway. "Did that bounder hurt you?"

Joia couldn't speak for the lump in her throat.

"He must have offered you some insult, then. Tell me and I'll thrash that dirty dish to an inch of his good-for-nothing life this time." Craighton had her hands in his now and was rubbing them, as if he could feel the chill that had invaded her, body and soul. Joia managed to shake her head in denial. Oliver hadn't insulted her; he'd only turned her world inside out.

"Dash it, what's wrong?" Comfort had witnessed wounded men behaving thusly, watching their own life's blood flow out of them. To see one of the most beautiful women in the world looking like she'd been gutshot wrenched at his own innards. He wanted to grasp Joia to him, to keep her safe. He wanted to wrap her in his arms so no one could hurt her ever again. Shocked by the unfamiliar surge of protectiveness welling up

36

in him, the viscount did, in fact, shake her. "Deuce take it, I thought you had more sense than to go off alone with that blackguard."

The shaking did what his sympathy couldn't. Joia found her voice. "I am going to marry the blackguard, my lord."

"What? You detest him. I've heard you and your sisters call him a maggot. You've hardly spoken to him all week, and that was after you left him stranded on a horse."

"Papa will be happy at the match."

"Will he?" He tipped her face up. "And what about you, my lady? You don't look like any radiant, blushing bride to me."

"I am the most . . . the most fortunate of females."

"Then why are tears running down your cheeks, sweetings?"

"They are tears of . . . of happiness."

By this time Joia was in Craighton's arms, sobbing against his chest. Usually he despised crying females. Usually they were weeping over some trifle or wheedling something out of him. Joia wasn't like that. She wasn't like any other female of his acquaintance. None that he knew would take to filling in their necklines with bits of lace and flowers. The silly goose hadn't realized that her efforts only drew a man's eyes to her endowments, she was such an innocent. Or was she? "That rotter hasn't compromised you, has he? Is that why you have agreed to marry him?"

"No, it's worse," she said with a sniffle, so he reached for his handkerchief, only then realizing he'd been holding his breath.

"Devil take it, if you're not breeding, there's no reason on earth to marry that loose screw." Who'd just escaped a death sentence. "Go to your father. He'll straighten out this mare's nest."

For answer he received another drenching. His damp coat had already soaked through to his shirt and skin. "Come on, sweetings, you're the one who said you'd never marry a man you couldn't trust. Surely you don't think Oliver will be faithful?"

He thought she whimpered something about no man being trustworthy, ever. That couldn't be, not with her father's example. Comfort had watched the earl and his countess this week and seen something so unique he hardly recognized it. The devotion between the couple was enough to make the viscount wonder what he'd been missing in his own life, make him wonder if such an abiding love was possible. His own parents lived on separate estates. If not for the war with France, they might live in separate countries. And hadn't he dallied with half the wives in London? What the Carrolls had was rare, rare and wondrous. It was no surprise that Joia wouldn't accept a marriage of convenience. Hadn't, until now.

"You cannot marry where your heart tells you no, Joia."

"You don't understand. I have no choice." She blew her reddened nose and wiped her swollen eyes.

Comfort thought she still looked beautiful. "So explain. I haven't had much practice slaying dragons recently, but I am willing to try."

"It's not your concern, my lord. You've already been more than kind. I . . . I must join the others at the modiste's."

"What, betroth yourself to rock slime, then go off to be fitted? Not so fast, my girl. Besides, I doubt you want to be seen on the High Street quite yet."

Joia dabbed at her eyes again. "Thank you, you're right. I'll just take a minute to compose myself. You needn't stay, my lord."

"You might try calling me Comfort, or Craighton. I've been known to answer to Craig in my salad days. I mean, after dousing a fellow's wardrobe, I should think you could be a tad less formal." When he saw the edges of her lips lift in the tiniest glimmer of a smile, Comfort casually added, "You do know, don't you, that I'll beat it out of Oliver if you don't tell me what's toward?"

"You can't!"

"I can and will, if you won't trust me."

Somehow she did. Her situation might be hopeless, but if there was anyone who could help, it was Comfort. He didn't even look so arrogant to her anymore, not with wet spots on his coat and his hair fallen in his face. Without thinking, she reached up to brush the misplaced curls back. He took her hand and brought it to his lips. "Tell me."

"Oliver knows a secret. It's a secret so terrible that my mother would be devastated if it were made public, which he threatens to do if I don't agree to announce our betrothal at the hunt ball. The scandal would destroy my sisters' chances to make good marriages. Then, when Oliver succeeds to the title, he'll make all their lives a living nightmare."

"A cad who threatens women will make life hell for them no matter what."

"Yes, I already assumed as much, but I have to try."

"You would sacrifice your own future, any chance for happiness you might have, for your mother and sisters?" Could any woman truly be so loyal, so generous? Comfort never thought such a female existed. In his experience, the prettier the chit, the more selfish. He gently kissed Joia's forehead, which seemed to be at the perfect height for such an homage. "I'll make it right, sweetings, see if I don't. If worse comes to worst, I'll call him out."

"But if you killed him, you'd have to flee the country. You mustn't do so on my account."

Comfort was beginning to wonder if there was anything he wouldn't do for Joia's sake. Obliterating Oliver seemed tame sport. "Don't worry, the twit might be treacherous, but he's too much the coward to accept my challenge. Besides, he cannot shoot. No, I'll try to find another way. We have two days before the ball, don't we? That's plenty of time to come up with an alternative plan."

"But not much time for a miracle."

"Chin up, sweetings, Saint George is riding to the rescue. In fact, there's another dragon that I need to be slaying for you, that worm who led you to this alley in the first place."

"No, getting rid of that particular reptile will be my pleasure."

Tom Beacon was shoveling manure. Tom Beacon was *always* shoveling manure. Mucking out twenty-odd stalls, twice a day, was no picnic. Now, with all the horses from the

Winterpark swells, he'd have another mountain of droppings to pick up and move. A bloke couldn't be blamed for trying to make the extra shilling or two, especially when his dear old mum was feeling poorly. Tom laughed to himself. His mother had left him on some church steps when he was an infant, or so he'd been told.

The laugh turned into a cough when he looked up to find Lady Joia standing at the gate of the stall he was cleaning. With insolent slowness, Tom pulled the filthy cap off his head. "What can I do for your ladyship now? Would you be wantin' your mare already?"

"What I am wanting is you gone from town. I'll never feel safe when you're around, you dastard."

Tom scratched his head. "Well, since I'm a free man and no highborn bitch can tell me where to go, I don't s'pose your feelings count for much."

Joia had her arms crossed over her chest. "And what about my father's feelings? He'll shoot you down if he gets wind of what you did. Then there's Mr. Humphreys, your employer, who put me on my first pony. One word from me and he'll take the horsewhip to you. I'd say my feelings, my right to get a peaceful night's sleep, count for more than your worthless hide. What do you think?"

"You can't do that!"

"I can, but I don't want your death on my conscience."

Tom was strong, but Humphreys was the blasted blacksmith. The mort had the right of it. "But me mum is sick an' she depends on me."

"Pond scum doesn't have a mother," Joia said, hitting too close to the truth for Tom's liking.

"But I didn't do nothin' wrong 'cept try an' earn some extra blunt," Tom whined, still trying to win her pity.

"At my expense. I can and will go to Humphreys if you're still here when my party returns for our horses. And don't think anyone else will help you or hire you, for the villagers all depend on Winterpark's patronage. I want you gone, far gone, where I never have to look on your foul presence again."

"But I ain't got coach fare, nor the blunt to rent a horse.

Ain't been at the livery long enough to get paid, even. I been lucky to get room an' board."

"Your luck just changed." Joia reached into her reticule and pulled out a handful of coins and pound notes, which she tossed onto the nearest pile of manure. "You won't mind, I'm sure. Your hands are already dirty."

Joia marched out of the stable, holding her skirts away from the dunghills, and her chin as high as a queen's. Comfort wanted to applaud from his position near the door. He'd been standing by, forcing himself to let the indomitable young woman handle the situation for herself. He knew she wouldn't welcome interference, just as he realized she needed to feel in command of something, anything, to restore her confidence and composure. Much as it went against his grain, Craighton was letting a willowy, wispy, not-quite-defenseless female fight her own battle. He'd allow her this skirmish, at any rate, as long as she was winning.

She'd departed triumphant, as the groom scrabbled in the manure heap for his buried treasure. The hedge bird would take the brass and fly, the viscount was sure, though he did intend to check back with the livery owner later. Comfort was about to follow Joia when he heard Tom mutter, "Bloody toffs. The French had the right of it."

So the viscount planted one well-shod foot on the groom's posterior and pushed. Saint George would be proud.

Chapter Six

*T*here was nothing the Earl of Carroll liked quite so much as a fine dinner among his family and friends, unless it was a cozy dinner with just his wife and daughters. Or a very private meal upstairs in their sitting room with his beautiful Bess. Tonight she was in some purplish taffeta gown that looked stunning with the amethysts he'd given her on their last anniversary. Damn if she didn't get more lovely every year. And damn this foolishness that had her at the opposite end of a long expanse of silver and centerpieces and serving dishes. Lord Carroll wanted to ask her opinion of the strange undercurrents he was sensing at the table. He'd just have to wait till later, he supposed, when they shared a last sip of wine before bed.

Something was afoot, though, he was sure. Joia hadn't joined the guests for sherry before dinner, and when she took her place at the table she was pale and unsmiling, turning down most of the dishes offered to her. Maybe the lass was sickening for something after all. Comfort kept staring at her from across the table, too, as though he was trying to send some kind of silent message, to the obvious displeasure of his dinner partner, that Willenborg female. The earl might have been heartened by Comfort's interest in Joia, but the chit never returned the viscount's glance. Lord Carroll supposed that meant they'd be going to London at the end of the month, yet again, dash it.

Blast, he groused to himself, Joia would never find a more eligible *parti*, and her poor father's gout was acting up, for all she cared. Of course, if the gout got so bad that he couldn't travel ... The earl signaled a footman to pour him another glass of wine, ignoring his wife's frown from the end of the table.

In contrast, that clunch Oliver was looking well pleased, though how a man could enjoy his meal with his shirt points poking him in the eye, Lord Carroll couldn't comprehend. Maybe Oliver's valet had found a golden boy in one of the noddy's pockets, for he wasn't getting any more funds from the estate to keep him happy, cousin's son or not. No, it was more likely that the gudgeon was in alt over a new waistcoat. The earl went back to his plate so he didn't have to look at the orange and green monstrosity.

The chef had outdone himself tonight. Lord Carroll couldn't decide if the lobster in oyster sauce was his favorite or the vol-au-vents of veal. Perhaps the—

Just then Joia jumped to her feet, tossed her napkin on the table, cried, "Papa, how could you?" and fled the dining room. With a nod from their mother, Holly followed her, begging the company's pardon.

Lord Carroll looked from his guests' shocked faces to his wife's equally dumbfounded expression. Then he looked down at the forkful of meat in his hand. "Damn, I thought she got over that nonsense about venison years ago. If we don't shoot the deer, they'll overrun the woods and start on the farmers' crops."

Neither sister returned to the dining room, nor were they in the drawing room when the gentlemen left their port and cigars to rejoin the ladies. Lord Comfort had the nagging notion that he'd find both venues equally as boring, without a certain blue-eyed beauty. He was quite disgusted with himself for automatically searching the room for Lady Joia when he came in, like a mooncalf. Obviously he must be coming on sick also, which had been the earl's excuse for his daughter's odd behavior.

Comfort knew better, and knew he had to act quickly before his damsel in distress gave in to the pressure of her cousin's threats. She was liable to announce the betrothal immediately, just to get the deed done, or else confront her father.

While he was closeted with the gentlemen, the viscount had studied his host, wondering about a scandalous secret that could destroy such a close-knit family. Joia's heart-wrenched "Papa, how could you?" certainly led one to guess the nature of the skeleton in Lord Carroll's closet, or its gender, at least. How could he? the viscount wondered, angry on the countess's behalf. Lady Carroll was the kindest, gentlest lady of his acquaintance, patently devoted to her husband and daughters.

Infidelity might be the norm in tonnish marriages, but Craighton hadn't thought it was part of this marriage. His own mother never cared about her husband's numerous liaisons; Lady Carroll would care all too much, according to Joia and what he could see for himself. He wouldn't let Joia be forced into a loathsome match—he'd feel the same about any female being coerced, he almost convinced himself—but neither could he let the charming countess be hurt. He might just have to put a bullet through Oliver after all.

If that wasn't enough in his dish, the ripe young widow was eager to fall into his lap. Comfort could recognize the signs; the lady was growing impatient for him to make a move. Aubergine meant to snabble herself a title by hook or by crook. The near bare-breasted bait hadn't worked, so Lud knew what she'd try next. Comfort had a good idea, so he made sure his door was locked every night. He wasn't born yesterday, but he *was* born with women chasing after him.

"But what did Papa do to overset you so?" Holly wanted to know. She was standing by her sister's bedside, wringing out another towel soaked in lavender water to place over Joia's eyes. "Did he actually go ahead and accept some gentleman's offer for your hand without consulting you?"

Joia groaned. 'Twould have been better if he had, then Oliver couldn't make his vile proposal. She should have accepted Lord Hopworth last year, drool and all. No, then Oliver would only blackmail Holly, the next daughter in line. Joia groaned again.

"Surely he didn't refuse someone you were interested in, for I think Papa would approve Mr. Humphreys's suit rather than go back to Almack's." When that effort didn't win her a smile, Holly tried a different tack. "No, the only gentleman remotely plausible is Lord Comfort, and Papa would be dancing for joy if he made you an offer, gouty foot or not. But you swore you'd never marry such a rake, didn't you?"

Joia groaned louder.

With Lady Carroll anxious to check on her daughters, the other ladies of the house party decided to retire early. Since Aubergine couldn't remain the only female downstairs, she was forced to seek her chamber, too, and just when she could have had the viscount to herself, without the Carroll chit to distract him. Pouting, she did manage to whisper him a hint that she'd never be able to fall asleep for ages yet. She'd welcome company, there in the fourth room on the right in the west wing with the other lady guests, in case he grew bored. Comfort gave a noncommittal smile as he bowed over her hand. It didn't take a genius to suspect he'd never leave that room without a pair of legshackles.

The gentlemen, not surprisingly, decided to play cards. The surprise was that Viscount Comfort invited Oliver Carroll to play piquet with him.

"I understand you are a prodigious player," his lordship said, either noting that Oliver was proficient with the pasteboards or commenting that he was a confirmed gambler. Since he was in such an expansive mood, Oliver chose to be complimented. He bowed, fluttering the ruffles at his throat and sleeves. "And we haven't had much opportunity to become acquainted, have we?" the viscount asked.

Since the only intercourse they'd had was the out-and-outer's fist hitting Oliver's cheek—purely by accident, Comfort swore—Oliver could only agree. His luck was certainly changing, with this plum landing in his plate. Why, the diamond in Comfort's neckcloth could pay off half of Oliver's creditors. No, Oliver decided, he could have the stone set into an engagement ring so he wouldn't have to waste good blunt on a gewgaw *he* wasn't going to wear. First, of course, he had to win the bauble, along with every other groat he could wring out of his high-and-mighty lordship's pockets. Oliver did not intend to lose.

Craighton was content to let the cards fall Oliver's way. He merely signaled the butler to refill their glasses of brandy. "You may as well leave the decanter here, my good man, for it looks to be a long night."

"I'll drink to that," Oliver seconded, raising his glass—and the stakes.

The two men stayed gaming long after most of the others had retired. A large pile of Comfort's cash was now on Oliver's side of the table, and Oliver was about to nudge him into putting the diamond stickpin there, too. Then Comfort's hand slipped. His brandy spilled all over the table and the cards. Oliver grabbed his winnings out of harm's way. The butler was there in an instant, mopping up, sweeping the ruined deck onto a silver dustpan.

"Terribly sorry, Bartholemew, isn't it? Must have had too much to drink. Better call it a night, eh, Carroll?"

Oliver was more than ready.

"As long as you promise me a rematch tomorrow night."

Oliver was even more ready for that. He'd never had a pigeon so ripe for the plucking, and here he'd thought Comfort was a downy bird. He whistled all the way up the arching marble staircase, and all the way down the east-wing corridor to his room across from Comfort's, not caring for those already asleep.

The viscount stayed below, helping the butler clean up the mess.

"This is not at all necessary, my lord," Bartholemew argued, his eyebrows raised to see a peer of the realm invade the butler's pantry, his private sanctuary, to wipe off a deck of cards.

"Oh, but it is, Bartholemew. Believe me, it is." Once the

cards were dried, the viscount inspected them more closely, looking for pinpricks or minute marks on the reverse sides.

"Ah, now I understand."

"Ah, indeed. Look at this. The edges have been shaved."

"I am not surprised. Master Oliver always was somewhat of a loose screw. Not what we can admire in the heir. Lord Carroll will have to be told, of course. Shall I?" The butler held his gloved hand out for the deck.

Instead, the viscount pocketed the evidence. "Not quite yet. I think I'd like to win back some of my blunt tomorrow, using an honest deck, before the earl gets involved. But first, I think you and I should have a little talk."

The butler's eyebrows rose even higher than before. "I'm afraid your lordship has indeed imbibed too freely this evening. Might I suggest a cup of coffee?"

"Excellent, and get one for yourself, because I'm afraid Lady Joia has a problem that I cannot help her solve without more information. In great houses like Winterpark, butlers of your long-standing tenure always know everything that's going on. They say a gentleman cannot keep secrets from his valet, but I've found them to be a fickle bunch, changing employers with the fashions. No, it's old family retainers like yourself who hold the confidences of their employers."

Bartholemew drew himself up in rigid affront. "I am sorry, sir, I do not gossip about the family."

"Would you rather see Lady Joia marry Oliver?"

"I'll get the coffee."

Chapter Seven

"*D*id you find out anything? Do you have a plan?" Lord Comfort knew Joia was really asking if there was any hope. They were out riding, visiting a few of the tenants. By pre-arrangement they had left before breakfast to keep Joia from having to give Oliver any kind of acknowledgment. The viscount also thought she'd be happier not facing her father over kippers and toast. Merry was along for propriety, but she and her dog were off on rabbit tangents.

Joia was as beautiful as ever in her military-style riding habit, but she still looked pale to Craighton, as if that leech Oliver were already sucking the life out of her. The viscount didn't feel so well himself, having stayed up half the night with old Barty. Once the venerable butler had unloosened, assured that Lord Comfort meant to aid the family against the encroaching Oliver, he'd grown positively voluble. Before Craighton had the information he wanted, he'd had two cups of coffee, then one with brandy, then half a bottle of Lord Carroll's finest cognac. Barty'd had the other half. The viscount hoped the old rascal felt half as bad as he did this morning.

"I learned a bit," Comfort told Joia now. "Did you know, for instance, that Oliver cheats at cards?"

Joia stopped along the leaf-strewn path to offer him a roll from the basket tied to her saddle. "He did as a child, so I'm not surprised he's still at it. I mean, a swine who would stoop to blackmailing his own family surely isn't above hiding cards up his sleeve."

"No, I wasn't surprised, either." Comfort held out an apple in exchange.

"What, did you play with him? I assume he's as bad a card-sharp as he is at everything else."

"Quite easy to detect, as a matter of fact."

She shrugged. "That's why he's never in funds, I suppose. So what will you do with your information? You did swear not to call him out, remember."

Comfort remembered no such promise, but Joia's worried look was gratifying to him. Of course, she might just care about him because he was helping her, but for now that was enough. "I thought of showing your father the shaved cards."

"What good would that do? Papa would throw Oliver out, but it wouldn't change anything. He'd still have his filthy secret and he'd be even more desperate for my dowry."

Killing the worm was beginning to seem the best course, but Comfort knew Joia wouldn't agree, so he tossed his apple core toward a chattering squirrel and said, "I found some information about your father, too."

"Never say he uses loaded dice." Joia's voice wavered. "Although I suppose nothing should surprise me anymore."

"Don't be ridiculous. Your father is a gentleman, an honorable, respected peer."

"And no peer cheats at cards?" she asked bitterly. "No gentleman cheats on his wi—" She didn't finish.

"I discovered some information, enough to judge the danger to your family, about an episode eight or nine years ago. I don't think the scandal would be as damaging as you assume. As you say, infidelity is not such a rarity among the ton. The gossip would be a nine days' wonder, is all. No one but the highest sticklers will be appalled by it."

"Mama will be."

The viscount rode alongside Joia, so he could take her hand. "I have every reason to believe that your mother knows. Wives usually do. Perhaps not all the details, but enough. And she has forgiven your father for his onetime lapse. Can you?"

"I . . . I don't know."

He took his hand away. "I was hoping you had more of your mother's loving-kindness, that could overlook a man's faults." He was wondering if she could forget about a man's past altogether.

Joia was wondering how a man could be so compassionate and still be a rake. Papa, of course. "How could she ever trust him again?"

"I believe that's where 'love conquers all' comes in. We'll never know, for I can't think you mean to question your mother about her feelings on the matter."

Joia didn't even want to examine her own feelings on the matter, so she changed the subject from men's pasts to her own future. "But what about Oliver and his poisonous threats? No matter what you say, I couldn't bear to see my family's dirty linen washed in public."

"Of course not. No, we have to defang the little viper. The fuzzed deck is a start, but I have some other cards up my own sleeve. Just avoid him for now and leave everything to me. The houseguests believe you are ailing anyway, so you should be able to keep out of his way without drawing comment. Especially with the ball tomorrow, they'll all think you are resting to regain your strength."

"But what about you? What are you going to do?"

"First, I intend to win my money back from our Captain Sharp. Then we'll see."

"That's your plan? Disaster is one day away and you are worried about your gambling losses?" Joia threw her apple, smashing it against an innocent tree.

Comfort drew his horse closer again, so his thigh brushed against her leg in the sidesaddle. "Now is the time to start learning to trust, sweetings. I'm not sure how the game will play itself out, but I swear that your family will not be hurt and you will not have to marry Oliver. I'll marry you myself, first."

Joia almost fell off her horse, but she wasn't as surprised as the viscount to hear those words come out of his mouth. "It won't come to that, I'm sure," he quickly added. "Trust me."

* * *

How many women had listened to how many men say, "Trust me"? And how many women had been disappointed by their handsome, smooth-tongued rogues? Joia had the headache for real. She didn't go down to dinner, to her father's perturbation.

Deuce take it, Lord Carroll muttered into his mutton. How the devil was a man supposed to enjoy his meal with all the intrigues going on? He knew there was some argle-bargle over Oliver. Dash it, there was always some disturbance when that cabbage head came to call. At least he didn't bother the maids anymore, after the housekeeper threatened to come after him with a butcher knife two summers ago.

According to Bartholemew, Viscount Comfort was handling the difficulty, which was, also according to the almost omniscient butler, a Good Thing. Barty thought Lady Joia might look more kindly on the raffish nobleman if he could perform this small service for her. Barty hoped for Great Things from that young man. Well, so did Lord Carroll, namely a grandchild, if his obstinate eldest daughter could be convinced to sit next to the chap. Instead she was taking to her bed, and the viscount was taking that blasted widow to his, from all appearances. Why, they were practically drinking out of the same cup at the dinner table. Why not? They were nearly sitting in the same seat. The eel in aspic tasted like ashes in Lord Carroll's mouth.

And there was worse news. Having informed the viscount of all that he thought the gentleman needed to know, Bartholemew had loyally reported to his employer all that he felt the earl needed to know. Joia, it seemed, had gotten an inkling of the Secret. Hellfire and tarnation, no wonder she'd been looking at her poor old father as if he'd crawled out from under a rock. The earl waved away the rack of lamb. Instead of losing his little girl to another man, which was hard enough for Lord Carroll to accept, he was losing her to his own folly.

All of the pieces were coming into place. Not necessarily the right place or the proper place, Comfort thought, so thank heaven Joia wasn't there to see him flirting with Aubergine

Willenborg. The widow was in black tonight, but if she was mourning anything, it was the loss of her underpinnings. The dress was so sheer, Craighton could swear she had nothing else on. If this were London a month ago, he'd have taken her somewhere to find out before the dessert course was served. Now the mousse was more tempting.

He must have given a convincing performance, though, from the sour looks he was receiving from the earl and the countess, their two youngest daughters, and the butler. Comfort wouldn't have been surprised if the chef came out to give an opinion of his behavior. Aubergine's opinion was obvious, as obvious as her charms. She was relieved. If she could get him into her bed, she could get him to the altar.

"But not your chamber, my goddess," Comfort whispered to her during Holly's masterful performance on the pianoforte after dinner. "It's too near the countess's, and I understand she is a light sleeper. No, you must come to mine in the east wing. If anyone sees you, say you were hoping Lady Carroll was still awake, for you need her opinion of your gown for tomorrow. My chamber is the second one down. I'll place a playing card under my door so you'll know which one."

"The knave of hearts, perhaps?" she cooed in his ear under cover of her waving fan.

"What else?" he answered, almost gagging on the heavy perfume sent wafting his way. Joia smelled of lilacs and lavender. "Oh, and you'd better wait an hour or so after everyone retires, my queen. I promised to teach young Carroll how to play piquet."

Oliver was eager to resume play as soon as the music was over. Craighton kept losing. He also kept signaling Bartholemew for refills of his and Oliver's wineglasses. On one of the butler's trips to their table in a secluded corner of the library, Comfort angrily gathered up the cards and tossed them onto Barty's silver tray. "Stap me if this ain't an unlucky deck," he drawled, falling back in his seat. "Bring us a new pack like a good chap."

"And some coffee, my lord?"

"What, are we out of cognac?"

When the butler left, sniffing his disdain, Oliver leaned toward the viscount. "Don't worry about old Prune Face. He disapproves of everything. I intend to put him out to pasture as soon as m'cousin sticks his spoon in the wall."

Comfort pretended to adjust his stocking to avoid Oliver's sour breath of stale wine in his face.

The new deck proved fortuitous indeed. The viscount started winning the occasional hand, then nearly every hand.

Oliver yawned. " 'Pon rep, it's past my bedtime. What say we continue the game tomorrow?"

"Can't quit now. Only honorable to let a chap try to recoup his losses when his luck is in. 'Sides, tomorrow is the ball. Got to do the pretty."

All of Oliver's financial troubles would be over then, so he agreed to play on. His opponent was drunk as a lord anyway. He couldn't win much longer.

Comfort could, and did. Oliver lost back this evening's gains and last night's, too. Still the viscount wanted to keep playing. "Give a certain lady time to get ready, eh?" he said with a wink, one man of the world to another.

Oliver kept playing and kept drinking along with his new boon companion. He kept losing, too. "Dash it, ain't it time to switch back to *my* lucky deck?" But the ever-efficient Bartholemew had told him that he'd taken that deck to the dustbin since the edges seemed a shade dog-eared. Oliver started signing chits.

"Are you sure, old man?" Comfort asked after the third or fourth.

Oliver waved his manicured hand. "M'cousin can't live forever, don't you know. Besides, you'll be wishing me happy soon enough, and the dibs'll be in tune then."

"Why, I'll wish you happy tonight," the viscount declared as he won yet another hand. "Barty, how about some champagne?"

Oliver didn't see Comfort's signal to the butler, and he didn't taste the powder that got mixed into his glass. He did hear the sum of his debts. "I . . . I don't feel quite well, my lord. You'll have to excuse me."

As soon as Oliver staggered off to his bed, shaking his head like a dog with water in its ears, Bartholemew placed a cup of coffee on the deal table. He placed Oliver's "lucky deck" beside it.

Craighton gathered up his winnings, leaving a neat stack of pound notes on the table that was beneath either man's dignity to notice or discuss. He held up Oliver's vouchers. "It seems I made myself a fortune tonight, Barty."

The butler shook his head. "I hope you don't grow as old as I am, my lord, waiting to be paid."

Comfort stood and put the marked deck in his coat pocket. "Oh, I fully intend to collect."

Then he went to his room and undressed, coat, waistcoat, neckcloth, shoes, and stockings. He debated about leaving his silk shirt, but compromised by undoing the topmost buttons. Over the shirt and his breeches he put on a maroon velvet robe. Then he opened his door and listened. Sure enough, he could hear Oliver snoring from the room across the hall. Pulling a card from the deck Bartholemew had handed him, the viscount slid it half under the door—of Oliver's room.

The card, of course, was the joker.

Chapter Eight

The screams came right on cue. First the viscount heard the whisper of—satin, he guessed from behind his own barely cracked door. Then a knob being turned. He'd have to tell old Barty the doors needed oiling. He couldn't make out the whispered endearments, just a soft murmur, but he could imagine the satin negligee drifting to the carpet, the white hand reaching to turn down the bedclothes, and the lush body gliding onto the bed, under the covers. Having played the scene so many times, Comfort didn't need to hear the widow's next lines, about how her darling could have stayed awake for her, could have left a lamp burning for her, could have welcomed her with a bit more enthusiasm. Mistresses always found something to complain about.

Aubergine wouldn't give up, not with so much at stake. She'd rouse her reluctant lover one way or the other. Craighton hoped Barty'd mixed just the right amount of the sleeping draught so Oliver got some pleasure out of the evening. It was going to be his last, unless matters were concluded to Comfort's satisfaction.

The clunch made either the wrong response or no response at all. The viscount thought he detected a ribbon of light from under Oliver's door and started counting. Two . . . three . . . A banshee's wail rang through the corridors of Lord Carroll's country home. Aubergine wasn't waiting for her maid to come cry rape or whatever she'd been planning; she brought the house down herself.

In case anyone missed the screech, and to cover up Aubergine's cries of "You sure as Hades aren't Comfort!" the viscount added his own efforts. "What's toward?" he shouted as if to his valet. "Are we under attack? Is the house on fire?"

Comfort's valet was long abed in the attics, but a voice down the hall picked up the call. "Fire? Did someone say fire?"

Doors opened, half-awake guests poured into the hall. The viscount made sure he wasn't the first in the corridor, so someone else had to say, "I think the screams came from this room."

As if he'd read the script, Lord Carroll thundered down the hall, nightcap bobbing, with his wife and daughters close behind. He pushed open the door to Oliver's room and raced inside.

"Bloody hell, Oliver. In your own family's seat? Have you no pride?"

Aubergine was beating the hapless Oliver over the head with a pillow. "You weren't supposed to be here, you jackass! This is Comfort's room!"

"Thought it was mine. Head's not quite right, don't you know." Oliver was having trouble focusing his eyes, and not just because of the drugged wine. Aubergine was stark naked. The pillow wasn't the only thing flailing about.

The chorus in the hall gave a collective gasp. One matron fainted. An ingenue giggled. Lady Carroll quickly ushered her daughters from the crowded room.

The viscount stepped forward, since everyone else seemed too stupefied to move, and handed the widow her robe. He was right; it was satin. He held it out, eyes averted, so Aubergine couldn't see his grin.

"Well, you've torn it this time, Ollie," Lord Carroll was shouting. "You'll marry the wench tomorrow, b'gad, because you're not heaping any worse shame on me and my house."

The word "marry" cleared Oliver's mind. "Can't do it, Cousin. Am already betrothed. Can't go back on my word as a gentleman."

The viscount was at Oliver's side of the bed, awaiting his turn. Now he leaned over and growled in the flat's ear: "Remember all those vouchers you signed? They're due tomorrow."

"Tomorrow? I can't—"

"I might be willing to forgive the debts if you do right by the lady."

The lady was doing some fast thinking herself. She'd been gulled, all right and tight, for which Aubergine couldn't even hold the viscount to blame. She'd planned on trapping him into matrimony, after all. Now she needed a husband in a hurry if she was ever to see the inside of a polite drawing room again. Oliver wasn't much of a specimen, but he was better than nothing. Besides, the viscount had proven too wily for her. Aubergine rather thought she'd prefer a husband with a weaker will, an emptier brain box. Oliver fit the bill. So what if he was a spendthrift and a gambler? He wouldn't get far with the tight hold she kept on her purse strings. The paltry fellow might be a nodcock, but he was going to be My Lord Nodcock, Earl of Carroll, someday. "Oh, Ollie," she cooed, patting his arm.

"No!" Oliver shouted, jumping off the bed like a scalded cat. "You can't do this to me. I'm supposed to get Joia." He pointed a shaking finger at Lord Carroll. "You can't preach propriety to me after what you've done. I'll tell everyone about the—"

Comfort grabbed a handful of the slug's nightshirt and lifted him clear off the floor, bony bare feet dangling in air. "Do you remember your 'lucky deck'? It's in my pocket, sirrah. You'll be hauled off to prison tomorrow, an' you don't wed the lady. Botany Bay, I don't doubt. A dainty chap like you mightn't even survive the passage."

Oliver's face was growing red from the constriction at his throat. He couldn't have answered if he'd wanted. Comfort gave him no chance, just another shake. "You'll marry the lady, and you'll keep your mouth shut. If I ever hear you've breathed one word to damage Lord Carroll's honorable reputation, I'll make sure you are never received anywhere, not in the clubs, not even in the lowest hells. Then I'll kill you, if Aubergine doesn't."

Comfort dropped Oliver to the floor and wiped his hands as if they were soiled. Lord Carroll was glaring at the onlookers to begone; the widow was tapping her foot impatiently. Oliver was already on his knees. He nodded and mumbled something about the happiest of men.

"There, now, that's all shipshape," the earl declared, not looking his wife in the eye as she led Aubergine back to her own room. "We'll hold the ceremony right before the ball tomorrow. Dashed if I'm going to give up my hunt for any wedding breakfast. And you deuced well better take a long honeymoon trip, out of my sight." He looked around to make sure his trusty butler was still in attendance. "We'll need a special license, Barty."

"The riders have been alerted, my lord. They merely await your signature on the letter to the archbishop."

"Good man. Oh, and put a footman outside the sapskull's door to make sure he doesn't shab off on his blushing bride."

"And one below his window, my lord. The men are already assigned."

"I daresay you and the viscount thought of everything." Lord Carroll couldn't keep the bitterness from his voice. They hadn't thought to tell him what was going on in his own home, as if he were too decrepit to be disturbed, or too senile to see to his own affairs. "I shall expect you, sir, in my office before breakfast tomorrow," he ordered the viscount. "Meanwhile, take your hands off my daughter, sirrah. I saw you panting after that trollop all night." He turned his back on them and marched down the hall, so they couldn't see the wink he gave Bartholemew. "Ten minutes ought to be long enough, eh?"

"Five, my lord. He's a bright lad."

"Were you?" Joia asked, still in Craighton's arms from their congratulatory hug, despite her father's orders. It only seemed natural to celebrate their success together.

"Was I what, sweetings?" Comfort was finding it difficult to concentrate with such a delightful armful, so near to his bedroom door.

"Were you panting after Aubergine, sir?"

"Only in the line of duty, I assure you. She is much too showy for my taste. Like some park prancer, all flash and no go."

"That's not what the *on dits* columns say."

"But it's what I say. I find I much prefer modest elegance to a brazen display." He was finding Joia, in her flannel gown buttoned to the chin, with a shawl over it to boot, infinitely more alluring than Aubergine in all her naked splendor. The widow's yellow hair reminded him of straw, while Joia's long golden night braid, so virginal, so innocent, begged a man to separate the tresses and run them through his fingers, to spread them on a pillow. This loyal and caring young woman stirred his blood like no dasher ever could. He didn't just want to take her to his bed, either. He wanted to take her to Ireland and to meet his mother. "There's a place for propriety, after all."

Propriety? Joia jumped back, out of an embrace she was enjoying much too much. His lordship would prefer whatever woman was in his arms at the moment, she feared. Still, he'd helped her and her family, so she mustn't appear ungrateful. She stood on tiptoe and kissed his cheek, which was the least of what she felt like doing. "Thank you, my lord. I don't know how I can ever thank you enough. I still cannot believe how you managed to get rid of Oliver so neatly."

The viscount grinned. "Brilliant if I have to say so myself. Of course, the inestimable Bartholemew deserves some of the credit, but none of your kisses, sweetings."

The corridor was too dark for him to see her blushes. "But to have the toad married, settled where he won't be able to bother any of us, where Aubergine will make sure he doesn't do anything to make himself persona non grata in Town, far exceeds brilliance. It's . . . it's miraculous."

"I told you I would save the day."

"Yes, but it seemed so hopeless and I—"

"Didn't trust me. Ah, my sweet, that's how you could thank me, with a little faith."

Joia was biting her lip, not knowing what to say. She wanted to tell him he was the most noble man she'd ever met, that his reputation no longer mattered. But it did.

And her obstinate refusal to see that a man could change bothered him. Still, he touched his finger to her lips. "Don't worry, Joia, we'll talk again tomorrow. You'll come to see what a steady fellow I am, if I survive the morning interview with your father."

"I'm sure he only wants to thank you for the service you've done all of us. He was just upset you didn't tell him of your plans."

"I think he was more bothered that you came to me with Oliver's threats instead of to him."

"I didn't precisely come to you, if you remember. You offered yourself."

Somehow the viscount's fingers were still at Joia's mouth, brushing her lips in butterfly caresses. "Sometimes I amaze myself." His own lips were about to replace his gentle touch, giving them both a glimpse of heaven, when Bartholemew cleared his throat. He and a footman were moving a chair down the corridor for the watchman set to guard Oliver's door.

"Wretched timing," the viscount muttered.

"Excellent timing," the butler countered, sending Joia flying down the hall in her bare feet, cheeks burning again.

"Wait!" the viscount called. "Will you save me the waltzes at the ball?"

"You saved me from Oliver, truly a fate worse than death. You may have anything you want."

Bartholemew opened the viscount's door for him. "Don't even think it."

"The waltzes will do. For now."

Chapter Nine

"*W*hat, are you riding to the hounds?"

Joia'd thought she'd be first in the breakfast parlor that morning, hurried along by anxiety over Lord Comfort's talk with Papa. Both of them, however, were before her, both in scarlet hunt jackets like her own wool habit, and neither showing any signs of agitation. Papa was already halfway through his gammon and eggs. She'd have to wait till later now, to find out what the men had discussed.

"My girls often hunt with the pack." Lord Carroll was answering the viscount's question. "And I don't care if it isn't considered proper in some corners. They're excellent riders all, mounted on the finest horseflesh my stables can provide, and they are aware of the limitations of the confounded sidesaddle, by George."

Joia usually turned back after the first few fields, enjoying the ride, the spectacle, the dogs, and her father's excitement, without any wish to see the poor fox slaughtered. Most times Merry stayed with the pack until the end, begging for a reprieve. When no one was about, when the fox had given them a good run, Lord Carroll would relent, for truth to tell, he admired the game little creatures himself. But today Reynard would have to depend on his own wits, for half the county was assembling in Winterpark's carriage drive and on the lawns, to Lady Carroll's dismay. The countess entered the morning room without her usual cheerful greetings. "If they trample my rhododendrons,

Bradford," she threatened, "there will never be another hunt at Winterpark."

Everyone knew she'd never deny the earl his favorite pastime, after raising horses and daughters, of course. While a footman poured her tea and brought a fresh rack of toast, Lady Carroll instructed Bartholemew to send out more trays of sweet rolls and stirrup cups to the eager, early riders outside. Of course, Bartholemew had already given orders to the kitchen, but the countess felt she had to do something before the rest of the company gathered to fortify themselves for their morning's run. In a bit she would go stand on the front steps waiting for the huntsman to blow his horn, to wave away the riders. Then she could come back and get down to the serious business of planning a wedding for the very afternoon of the hunt ball. Men! Did they never think?

Comfort thought Joia looked stunning this morning with her hair gathered back in a net and a tiny veiled hat pinned to her head. He also thought she might burst from curiosity, so, as the breakfast room filled, he went to the sideboard and brought back a plate of muffins, taking the seat beside her this time.

"What did my father want with you?" Joia asked, taking one of the proffered muffins onto her own plate. "Was he very angry? Did you tell him about Oliver's blackmail scheme?"

Comfort was buttering his muffin. He noted that Joia preferred jam on hers. "He was furious at Oliver, of course. I thought he had a right to know in case the dastard tries to extort money or something from your family again. I think the earl is going to offer a honeymoon in Austria to Mrs. Willenborg as a wedding gift. The beau monde is gathering there, which ought to please Aubergine, and it's far enough away that your father won't have to lay eyes on the makebate or his bride."

"And was that all Papa had to say?" To avoid Comfort's eyes, Joia gave her muffin another dab of jam.

"I think that was the gist of it. Oh, he did give me permission to ask for your hand in marriage."

'Twas a good thing they were having strawberry jam today. The stains wouldn't show on Joia's habit. "Botheration, that's what I was afraid he'd do! With Oliver out of the running, you're his last hope for the house party."

"Never say so. I understand your father invited half the Horse Guards barracks up from London for the ball tonight."

"But I understand the odds are heavily in your favor," she teased back. "Why, the underfootman couldn't find anyone to take his bet. I'm sorry, my lord. I know you never intended . . . That is, pay no mind to Papa's schemings."

"Not at all, sweetings. I asked him."

Joia's hand stopped between the plate and her mouth. "You asked him what?"

"Permission to pay my addresses, of course."

Joia threw her hands in the air. Unfortunately, she hadn't put the muffin down first. Now there were stains on Comfort's clothes as well, and Lady Carroll was scowling from her end of the table. "Why did you do a hen-witted thing like that?" Joia demanded. "Now he'll never stop badgering you."

"I asked him because it's the proper thing to do. I don't mean to put my luck to the touch yet, though, so you needn't give me any answer yet. I thought we should get to know each other better. What do you think?"

Joia couldn't think. Her brain had turned to strawberry jam.

Joia didn't see the viscount again until after the wedding. That is, she saw him—he rode at the forefront of the hunt; she turned back at the home farm—but not to speak to, certainly not to demand if he'd contracted a brain fever. What other explanation could there be for his latest faradiddle? He couldn't be serious, she told herself. Could he? He was kind and chivalrous once he got off his high horse, good company and surprisingly good-natured, but he wasn't ready to set up his nursery; he'd said so himself. And he didn't like proper young women; he'd said that, too. Joia didn't know what she'd do if he'd changed his mind, nor what she'd do if he hadn't. What a muddle!

The wedding was almost as chaotic as her thoughts. As if the household and the neighborhood weren't set on their collective heels already, Aubergine insisted Viscount Comfort give the bride away, just to roil the waters. She saw the way the wind was blowing and had no reason to provide the viscount smooth sailing, not after the trick he'd played on her.

"By Jupiter, I swear she was never mine to give," Comfort told anyone who would listen. "I had my heart set on being groomsman."

The earl took that honor, standing by Oliver's side, making sure his unworthy heir made the right responses without shabbing off at the last minute. He might have had a pistol in his pocket directed at the clunch's head, for all Oliver's joy in the occasion. Instead Lord Carroll had a ring in his pocket, the gaudiest trinket in the family vault, where it had lain for ages, the thing was so ugly. Aubergine loved every diamond, emerald, and ruby in the monstrosity.

The widow had refused to have Joia as bridesmaid. "I'll be dashed if I'm going to be overshadowed by some milk-and-water miss on my own wedding day. It's bad enough the groom's finery outshines anything I own. I'll have the middle gel—what's her name?"

Joia resented the implication on her sister's behalf, so she spent the afternoon convincing Holly to remove her spectacles, do her hair up in a more modern style under Joia's own diamond tiara, and touch her cheeks with the hare's-foot brush. In her ecru gown, Holly looked more like a bride than Aubergine. Her dance card for the ball that night was filled before the first wedding toast was given.

There weren't many—toasts, that is. Even the smooth-tongued viscount was hard put to come up with a polite way of saying he hoped the two didn't murder each other before the honeymoon was ended. He did hand Oliver the packet of his IOUs to burn as a wedding present.

Then, mercifully, the newlyweds were on their way, with at least five people thinking what Merry put into words: "Good riddance to bad rubbish."

In a few hours the house party would gather again for dinner, before the outside guests arrived for the ball. The ladies were going upstairs to rest and repair their toilettes. The gentlemen were headed to the billiards room, to recount the day's run one more time.

Lord Carroll stopped Joia on the stairs. "I'd like to have a word with you, puss. And your young man."

"He's not my young man, Papa, and I really don't have time. My hair . . ."

"Is perfect, as always. If you make yourself any prettier, I'll have to beat your beaux off with my cane. Let Holly shine tonight."

"Holly always shines, Papa."

The earl's chest expanded in pride. "She does, doesn't she? Deuce take it, though, did you see her this afternoon? I'll have mooncalves littering the doorstep knee-deep. When did she grow up, I wonder? I always knew she'd be a beauty, with brains to boot. But enough of that. I have something that needs saying to you today, something that won't keep any longer."

"It's all right, Papa. You don't need to explain anything."

"You almost married Oliver over it. I want you to understand what happened."

"It's not *my* understanding you need."

"No, but perhaps it's what you need, my dear, before you think of taking a husband, or refusing one."

Comfort was already in the library, gazing at the flames in the fireplace when they came in, looking magnificent in his dark evening clothes with his dark hair combed back. Joia liked it better when the thick waves fell in his forehead. He didn't seem so toplofty then. She wished Papa would speak his piece and begone, so she could find out what Comfort had meant—and perhaps muss his hair the slightest bit.

"Are you too warm?" He misinterpreted the betraying blush on her cheeks. "Shall I bring you some wine?"

Lord Carroll stared at his own glass for a while, gathering his thoughts. "I have always loved your mother, Joia," he finally said. "And I never strayed from her except that one time."

Joia started to rise. "I don't want to hear this, Papa."

But Comfort took her arm and bade her sit. "We should listen."

"There was a funeral," the earl began. "It doesn't matter whose, I hardly remember, but I had to attend. One of you girls was sick, the measles or the croup or heaven knows what, and your mother did not want to leave you, so I set out alone. It was wintertime and the roads were terrible, all muddy and rutted, then iced over so you couldn't see the craters." He sipped at his wine, remembering.

"There'd been a coaching accident on the road, and I told my driver to pull over and see if any of the passengers needed assistance, even though it was late and I was eager to get home to my wife and sick children. The coachman said his guard had ridden for help, but there was one lone female on board, and could I take her up and out of the cold, as it was beginning to snow again. Of course, I did. She was a drab little squab of a thing, a schoolmistress returning to the girls' academy where she taught. She was nigh frozen and her lips were blue, so I offered her my flask, which seemed to help.

"By the time we reached the inn the coachman had directed us to, the snow was falling harder, so I decided to spend the night there also. I made sure Miss Applegate had a room and dinner and a hot bath, and I sent up another bottle of wine, because she'd been so chilled. Then I proceeded to have my own dinner in the private parlor, and to drown my loneliness in the host's smuggled brandy."

"But you never drink to excess, Papa."

"Not anymore, I don't. I'm not saying it's an excuse. A man has no excuse getting cup-shot if he's going to lose control. And that's what happened. You see, the wantwit of an inn-keeper thought Miss Applegate was my ladybird—saddest excuse for a bird of paradise I ever saw—and put her in my room. I went up, more than a shade castaway, undressed in the dark, and threw myself on the bed—on top of Miss Applegate. Well, she started screaming, so I kissed her, to shut her up. Then she was crying. Seems she'd never had strong spirits before. Anyway, I held her, and one damn fool thing led to another. I was horrified when I woke up to find a strange woman asleep in my bed. Almost as horrified as I thought the schoolmistress was going to be, so I took to my heels before dawn. I hired a carriage to take her to the school, and left her my card. Three months later I received a letter from her. She was breeding. She was about to be turned off without any family to go to, without a reference, without a brass farthing. Who would hire an instructress no better than she ought to be, much less one with a child? How could I abandon a young woman and an innocent babe? Would that have been the honorable thing to do?"

It might have been the wiser, but Joia had to shake her head no.

"I sent her funds to rent a cottage, and then found the infant a foster family so she could resume her life, short though it turned out to be. I never saw her again, I swear it. I had to tell your mother because I couldn't live with the guilt."

"How could she trust you again after that?"

"I gave my word."

"But you'd given it before, when you said your marriage vows!"

"And I meant them, dash it! One night, one mistake, out of twenty years? Your mother knows I'd never stray again. I couldn't live with myself for the hurt I brought her, and now you. She forgave me, puss. Can you?"

Joia looked at her father, whom she'd adored all her life, gazing at her so hopefully. So he couldn't part the seas, he was still her father, and she didn't love him any less. Then she looked over at Comfort and knew why he'd wanted her to listen to Papa's tale. His past wasn't spotless either. Trusting a rake was going to take a giant leap of faith.

"I'll try, Papa. I'll try."

Chapter Ten

$\mathcal{L}$ady Carroll had exceeded herself, the county agreed at that night's hunt ball. Winterpark glowed with beautiful flowers and beautiful women. The food was delicious, and the gossip was even better.

Any of the houseguests present for the wedding ceremony was a sage. Anyone present at the bumblebroth in Oliver's bedroom was a celebrity.

Now all eyes were on Joia and the viscount as they enjoyed their second dance together. Since it was only the second set of the evening, speculation was rife. The first had been the cotillion. As one of the highest-ranking gentlemen, it was Comfort's duty to lead off the eldest daughter of the house, behind the earl and countess. The second dance was a waltz, which the viscount had already appropriated and refused to relinquish. They both knew that one more dance together would be tantamount to a declaration, even by country standards, but they still hadn't found time to hold a private conversation.

"Do you think it's too cold for a stroll on the patio?" Comfort asked, reluctant to hand Joia over to her next partner. Tall and slim, dressed in lace-trimmed burnt orange with her golden hair in wisps about her face, she reminded him of a wavering candle flame, beckoning, warming, mesmerizing. There was no way in hell he was passing her on to some cake in overstarched shirt collars. "We should speak."

Joia didn't think a stroll through the Antipodes would be too cool, not after being held in Craighton's arms through the waltz. She did borrow Merry's paisley shawl, which her youngest sister had brought along to liven up her pale yellow gown, as though Merry's red curls and laughing eyes needed any more animation.

Joia made sure to avoid her mother's glance, but she did catch Papa's nod in Comfort's direction.

"He *is* pushing you into this!" she said on their way through the French doors.

"Who is pushing me into what, my sweet?" Comfort asked, more interested in making sure they were out of sight of the curious eyes than anything else. He led her toward a path where the nearby rosebushes bore their last, late blooms, warmed by the protection of the house. Fairy lights, paper lanterns hung in the trees, lighted their way.

"My father, of course. He's talked you into one of those dratted dynastic marriages where two great estates and fortunes come together. You need an heir, Papa wants a titled son-in-law. *Voilà!* A match is made. Well, I say no!"

Comfort had his arm on Joia's shoulder, to make sure she didn't stumble. He pulled her closer to his side, but kept walking. "Do you know, my lady, I believe you have just rejected the second offer of marriage that I didn't make. Terrible habit you have."

Joia couldn't tell if he was smiling there in the shadows, but she thought he must be. And he wasn't angry, for he didn't remove his arm. "That kind of marriage is just what I don't want."

"Ah, now we are getting somewhere. What *do* you want, sweetings?"

"I want love and affection and passion, all wrapped together. I want a man to want to marry *me*, not what I can bring to a marriage. I want—"

Whatever else she wanted would have to wait as Craighton brought his other arm around her and drew her against his chest for a kiss that had the Chinese lanterns doing somersaults.

"Is that enough passion, my love?" he whispered into her mouth, his hand stroking up and down her back, under Merry's shawl. "If not, I could . . ." His hand moved to her side, just beneath her breast.

"No! I mean yes." The hand moved higher, during another senses-stirring kiss. "I meant I thought it was enough." Joia knew her wits had gone begging, especially when she had to bite her tongue to keep from begging for yet another kiss. "But . . . but that's not all."

"Lud, much more and I'm like to expire, sweetings," Craighton said, trying to catch his own breath. "Whatever happened to Miss Prunes and Prisms?"

Joia sighed. "She's still here. I still want constancy in a husband, a man I can depend on."

"Ah, here's the crux, then. If I promised not to stray, would you believe me? What if I said that I've seen what your parents have—even with the misadventure—and decided that only their kind of marriage will do for me, too, the forever kind, the sharing and caring kind? What if I told you that I waited to marry until I found the one woman who makes my heart sing, so no other song will do?"

"Am I the one? Are you sure?"

For answer he put her hand against his heart. "It's playing a waltz, our waltz, Joia. Can you hear it?"

She rather thought the strains of a quadrille were drifting through the ballroom doors. "Do you truly love me, then?" She hadn't dared to hope.

"It's like seeing snow for the first time. I didn't know such a thing was possible, my joy. You showed me. And if you don't love me that much yet, well, I mean to make you. What would it take, slavish devotion, slaying more dragons, letting your sisters trounce me at jackstraws?"

"I think one more kiss ought to do it, for I've loved you forever."

One kiss wasn't nearly enough for either of them, of course. When the viscount needed to breathe, he told Joia, "You'll never have to worry about my being unfaithful, for I never intend to be away from your side. You'll have me next to you by day and in your bed every night."

That sounded appealing to both of them, but Joia had to ask,

"What, am I to be your warden to keep you honest, your keeper?"

"You're already the keeper of my heart. Nothing else matters."

Some time later, the viscount took his arms away and stepped back. "No, no more until we are married or your father will have my head. That marriage had better be dashed soon, sweetings, I'm warning you now."

Joia pretended to think a moment. "Do you know, I don't believe I ever heard a proper proposal?"

"What, should I give you a chance to reject me a third time? Never. Besides, I have it on good authority that the proper Lady Joia would never give her kisses where she doesn't intend to give her hand."

With that he led her back to the ballroom, where the orchestra was playing another waltz. "It will be our third dance, my love. Shall we?"

"I am sorry, my lord, but I do believe that all of my waltzes are promised to a devilishly handsome rogue with a wandering eye and a wicked reputation."

"That chap's been put to grass. You'll have to take me."

She laughed. "Since that seems to be the best offer I'm like to get, yes, my love, I will."

Since all eyes had been on the door waiting for the couple's return, everyone at the ball noticed that a lock of the meticulous viscount's hair had fallen in his face, that the fashionable Lady Joia wore a pink rose in her hair that clashed quite horribly with the orange of her dress. And that they danced as if no one else were in the room.

Lady Carroll made sure she was standing near their position when the music ended. She tried to look severe over such a lapse in decorum, but failed when the viscount kissed her hand and swore to cherish her daughter for a lifetime, at least, for she had made him the happiest of men.

"Then I am happy, too, my lord." The countess wiped a tear from her eye.

"What's this, eh?" Lord Carroll was there, holding out his

handkerchief. "This should be a joyous time, what? Instead my Bess is turning into a watering pot."

Joia's sisters had left their dance partners to come see what was toward, and they were teary-eyed, too, Holly making a pretty speech about welcoming their new brother-in-law, but Merry simply throwing her arms around the viscount's neck, to her mother's chagrin.

The earl shook his head. "Never try to make heads nor tails of a woman's reasoning, my lad. And always carry extra handkerchiefs."

Lady Carroll clucked her tongue. "Bradford, are you trying to frighten the poor boy off before there's even been an announcement?"

"An announcement, that's what we need!" the earl declared, on the off chance that his hard-to-please daughter might change her mind. "Not that there isn't a soul in the room who hasn't figured it out for himself. We'll need some—"

"Champagne, my lord?" Bartholomew appeared at Lord Carroll's elbow with a tray and full glasses, while similarly burdened footmen circulated throughout the vast ballroom. "We were prepared for a Great Event."

"Excellent man. You should be running the government, except what would we do without you here at Winterpark?"

"I am sure I couldn't say, my lord."

"Yes, well, it didn't take an Aristotle to figure this one out, what with these two smelling of April and May."

"June," the countess declared, downing her second glass of champagne. "We'll have a beautiful June wedding at Saint George's, Hanover Square. I suppose we'll have to invite the Prince and his brothers, but perhaps they won't come. The reception will be at Carroll House, of course; the gardens should be at their prime, especially if we start early in the spring. I can almost see the wedding in my mind, Joia dear."

Lady Carroll was slightly on the go, and who could blame her, with her house turned into a gabble-grinder's banquet hall? What with Oliver's mingle-mangle, Joia's making mice-feet of her reputation, and the hint of old scandals on new lips, it was no wonder the countess forgot herself. Of course, she could see that June wedding, for it was the one she'd planned for herself twenty years ago. "It will be the wedding that I never got to have."

"Whyever not, Mama?" Joia asked the question they were all wondering. "It's not as though you made a runaway match."

"Why is your anniversary in February if you dreamed of a June wedding?" Holly wanted to know.

Lady Carroll giggled. "Because the date had to be moved forward."

"Now, Bess, there's no need to go into past history."

"Why not?" the countess asked, fluttering her husband's handkerchief in his direction. "Every other family secret seems to be public knowledge."

"Mama! Never say you and Papa anticipated your vows!" Holly exclaimed, while Merry's jaw fell open.

Joia was doing some calculating. "But that makes me—"

"The eldest daughter." Craighton hurriedly filled the breech, waving off Bartholemew and his refilled tray of champagne. "And I am sorry to disappoint you, my lady, but I shall need to be in Ireland in the spring, to see about the new foals. No sense putting all the money and effort into the venture if I'm not going to be there. And I did promise Castlereagh I'd attend the meetings in Vienna this winter. He's a friend of my father's, you know. I thought, that is, Joia and I decided to wed soon, and honeymoon in Vienna. We could keep an eye on Oliver, too."

Lady Carroll started weeping again. "Now, Bess, you know youngsters get impatient." Lord Carroll frowned toward his youngest daughter, who had to clamp her hand over her mouth to keep from laughing. "And a Christmas wedding is everything magical. We can hold a ball. . . ."

"We hold a ball every Christmas, Bradford."

"Yes, but this will be the finest. We'll invite everyone, even the mad king; you'll spend a fortune, turn Winterpark inside out, and dress the girls in silks and velvet."

"I'm not having my daughter's bridal gown made by any provincial seamstress, Bradford."

"Of course not, my dear. The Carroll ladies will be dressed

by the finest modiste in the land. I expect nothing less." He expected to have to sell some Consols to pay for it all.

"Then it will have to be London, and you'll come along, too, Bradford. There are bound to be engagement balls, and Carlisle is usually in London for the Little Season. His Grace will want to meet our Joia. And Meredyth can use a little Town bronze if she's to be presented next spring."

"Comfort, be a good chap and find me a chair. Damn gout is paining me something dreadful."

Chapter Eleven

$\mathcal{J}$oia and her new fiancé watched her parents climb slowly up the staircase after the last guests had left or retired to their rooms. The ball had been an unqualified success, especially once the champagne started flowing, but now they were all weary. The earl was leaning on his walking stick between stairsteps, and the countess had a handkerchief pressed to her forehead to stop the pounding there.

"Do you think they are happy about the wedding?" Joia asked, taking a step closer to Craighton's side now that her parents' backs were turned.

He smiled down at her and put an arm around her waist. "I think your father is in alt, except for the London trip, and your mother will have the affair organized down to the last flower by tomorrow afternoon. She'll be even more resigned as soon as she has a grandchild to spoil."

"So long as that happy event comes none too soon," Joia added, showing her dimples. "Poor Mama couldn't take another shock to her notions of propriety."

"Little chance of that happening," Comfort noted dryly, nodding toward where Bartholemew was fussing over a stain on the Queen Anne table in the hall. They were out of the old retainer's hearing but in his sight, along with the tall pendulum clock he kept glancing at, none too subtly.

Barty would just have to give them a few minutes more, Comfort decided. A fellow didn't get betrothed every day. It appeared, however, he would be going to bed unfulfilled every night until that blasted wedding. "Most of all, they want your happiness. Does a December wedding please you?"

He was hoping she'd say no, they should marry as soon as the banns could be read, but of course, his decorous darling would never entertain such forward thoughts.

"I suppose Mama would have kitten-fits if we ran off to Gretna Green tomorrow. Two months seem such a long time to wait."

He chuckled. "Elopements are not at all the thing, my sweet, but definitely tempting. Speaking of tempting, you'd best begone before I forget myself."

Comfort thought he heard Bartholomew sigh in relief, but he was too busy kissing his newly betrothed good night to chide the old man for listening. Then he didn't care who was listening, or what he heard.

The kiss left both Joia and her viscount so unsatisfied, so yearningly hungry for more, that sleep would be elusive. So they shared another embrace, to dream on. And another, because it was going to be a long night apart.

Bartholomew stifled a yawn. It was going to be a very long two months.

"Do you think they'll be happy?" The Earl and Countess of Carroll were having their ritual last sip of wine in the sitting room between their chambers. With few exceptions, they'd shared this moment for over twenty years, speaking of their daily joys and sorrows, their plans for tomorrow, without interruptions by servants or children. Ready for bed in robes and nightgowns, they sat side by side on the sofa in front of the dying fire, Lord Carroll's foot propped on a stool in front of them.

Lady Carroll was sipping tea instead of wine, and she was frowning. "Neither can back out after tonight, Bradford, you know, not without bringing disgrace to both of them. Joia would be labeled a flirt and a jilt, in addition to being hard to please, and Comfort would be so dishonored, no respectable female would welcome his addresses. Except for fortune hunters, of course, or mushrooms."

The earl patted his wife's hand. "Don't get in a fidge, Bess, they suit to a cow's thumb. They couldn't be a better match than if I'd planned it myself."

"You did plan it, shameless conniver that you are. I saw all those worthless suitors you trotted out for Joia's inspection. Dear Comfort had no competition."

The earl laughed, caught out. "The lad would have shone no matter who else was in the running. Breeding, don't you know."

"Charm, more like it. But two months to plan a wedding, Bradford! It will be a skimble-skamble affair, to be sure. Why, the church in Carrolton cannot seat half our friends and relatives, as is, to say nothing of Comfort's family. And you know the duke and duchess have to be seated in separate pews."

"It's winter, Bess, not everyone will come. You can pray for snow," the earl said, showing complete lack of consideration for how that would throw off all his wife's plans and calculations. "Besides, my love, isn't it more important that Joia and Comfort be together?"

"I simply wish they'd known each other longer before making the announcement," she insisted, sipping at her tea.

"I knew you were the one for me the first moment I laid eyes on you, Bess. Do you remember? 'Twas at Lady Skippington's ball. You were all in white, with acres of skirts, and your hair was powdered and piled on top of your head."

"I was so terrified, I must have looked like a ghost in all that white! I was afraid that my father would force me to marry you because you were such an advantageous match." She studied the inside of her cup. "I didn't love you at first, you know."

"No?" He'd heard the tale before.

"But then you smiled."

"And you smiled back. You were the most beautiful creature I'd ever seen. You had a rose in your hair that perfectly matched the color of your lips. I wanted to kiss them right then, when your father introduced us. So I kissed your hand instead."

"I was petrified of doing something schoolgirlish and giving you a disgust of me. You were so elegant by comparison, so sophisticated."

"So old, you mean. What had I, a thorny old bachelor at six and thirty, to do with such a tender bud?"

"Everything, dearest, for you know I never wanted any other beau but you after that night."

"And we've been happy, even without that spring circus of a wedding."

Lady Carroll had to acknowledge that no, the size of the wedding was no reflection on the strength of the marriage. Their Graces of Carlisle's wedding was more like a coronation, and they'd lived apart since the birth of the heir. "Somehow we've managed, despite such a hole-in-corner affair."

"That still cost your father an abbey. We were lucky, weren't we?"

She sighed and rested her head on his shoulder, thinking of the past twenty years they'd had together, and their three daughters. So many couples had so much less. "Very lucky."

"But I'm getting old, Bess."

"Never say it, Bradford. Your foot is just paining you. I told you to stay away from those lobster patties."

"No, my love, it's true. More of my schoolmates have their names in the obituaries than in the *on dits*. You're as beautiful as ever, Bess, and I'm an old man."

"Nonsense, you're still elegant and sophisticated, more so, in fact, now that your hair has become such a distinguished silver. Why, I thought you the most handsome gentleman at the ball tonight."

"Doing it too brown, my dear, but thank you." He carried her hand to his lips and placed a tender kiss on the palm. "And you were the most beautiful lady there. Did I tell you how becoming you looked in that claret color? It's quite my favorite on you, you know, except when you wear blue, to match your bonny blue eyes. Or pink like this gown you have on"—he touched the silk at her neck—"that makes you look eighteen again. Ah, Bess, I should have let you marry a younger man so you wouldn't be alone, but I was too selfish. I cannot regret that."

"I am *not* alone, Bradford."

"Of course not, Bess, and I don't intend to stick my spoon in the wall any time soon. When I'm gone you'll have the girls, and a fine son-in-law, too. Perhaps grandchildren."

She rubbed his cheek with the back of her hand. "You're all I want, Bradford. And you mustn't worry about me."

"But I do. Your settlements are secure and I've made investments in your name, but Oliver—"

Putting her fingers over his lips, Bess said, "Oliver is your heir, and there is naught you can do about it. Talking yourself into the blue devils is foolish, especially on such a happy occasion as this."

"But what if there were something that I—that we—could do about Oliver?"

The countess laughed. "We would have done it years ago. It's not as if we didn't try, my love, or have you grown too old to remember?" she teased.

"I'll show you how much I've forgotten in a minute, you saucy wench, but first I want to have my say. It's about the boy."

"What . . . ? Oh, that boy." The countess put her teacup down and moved to the end of the sofa. "You swore we need never discuss that again, Bradford."

"But things are different now, Bess. Oliver knows, and Comfort. And all the girls, I suppose. Nothing stays secret in a place like this, by Jupiter."

"And who will broadcast our shame, now that Oliver has been silenced? No one will wash our dirty linen in public, Bradford, so there is no need for you to concern yourself. Or me. Do not, I beg of you, mention that . . . that child again."

He leaned over, but she was out of reach, stiff and unyielding. "Ah, Bess, I thought you forgave me."

"I did, Bradford, I forgave you then, and I forgive you now for letting that . . . that affair almost ruin Joia's life, and all of our reputations. But I cannot forget, my lord, and you must not remind me. For that matter, I do not need to be reminded that you are left with your cousin's boy as heir because I did not manage to provide you with a son. I tried, my lord, so help me I did. I wanted more than anything in this world to give you what you wanted."

"Now, Bess, I never held you responsible for that!" he exclaimed, dismayed to see tears in his beloved's eyes again that night. "May as well blame my brother Jack for dying before he left an heir, or my father, for not having more than the two sons to carry on the title. I never, ever blamed you." He held his arms out, but she did not return to his embrace.

"No, you never said anything." The countess spoke softly, remembering old pain. "But I could tell how discouraged you were each time I presented you with a daughter."

"Deuce take it, I'd not trade a one of my angels for any number of bothersome boys, and you know it."

"I also know how disappointed you were when the doctor said he didn't think there'd be any more children after Meredyth. And when he was proved right. I know you despise Oliver, Bradford, and would do anything to cut him out of the succession. I don't even blame you, after what he's done. But you cannot! Certainly not with . . . with that woman's son, so please do not speak of him to me again." She stood and gathered her robe more closely around her, pretending there weren't tearstains on her cheeks. "And now I have the headache, my lord. I know you will understand and excuse me. It has been a long day."

The earl understood all too well: he'd be sleeping alone tonight, confound it. Lord Carroll had a few good years left in him, and by George, he meant to spend a goodly portion of them in his wife's bed.

She'd come around soon enough, he knew. Bess's tempests blew themselves out quickly. By tomorrow she'd be rapt in her lists of what to purchase in London, what to have refurbished at home, consulting with him when they all knew Bartholemew made all the decisions. The hidden hurt would remain forever, he supposed in regret, but she'd bury tonight's anger in the depths of tomorrow's details.

But the earl couldn't forget about the child, or his plan to bring him home. His Bess had a warm heart, he knew she did, and big enough for one little boy, if only he could reach it.

Meantime, his own bed loomed all too big, and all too cold.

PART TWO

Beaux of Holly

Chapter Twelve

$\mathcal{H}$olly pushed the spectacles farther up her nose. Joia might be correct that her sister looked better without them, but Holly definitely saw better with them, especially nearby things like the chess set. Besides, no one was here to notice her looks one way or the other except Papa. Usually Holly needed every advantage she could find when playing against her father, but today the earl did not seem to be concentrating. "What is it, Papa? Is your foot bothering you again?"

"What's that, poppet, my foot? No, no, just wool-gathering. I expect we should have stayed on in London."

"You're missing Mama, is all. You know she had to stay in Town for the final fittings of Joia's wedding gown and to purchase the rest of her trousseau. There is the party at Princess Lieven's, also. Mama couldn't very well slight the Russian ambassador, could she?"

"Of course not, when the do's in Joia's honor. Still, I hadn't ought to have dragged you back to Winterpark two weeks early, just because my gout was plaguing me."

"What, I should have stayed for yet another affair where one waits an hour to make one's curtsy, then spends an hour trying to leave the premises through the hordes of other guests? Two weeks of that was enough to last a lifetime, though I suspect Mama will have us all back in Town in the spring."

They both sighed.

"But all females love shopping," the earl said, moving to

protect his queen. "I shouldn't have taken you away from all that."

"You didn't abduct me so you'd have a chess partner, Papa. I begged Mama to let me accompany you. Since Madame Celeste already has my measurements, even she agreed there was no call for me to spend endless hours being poked and prodded. No, thank you, Papa, I'd much rather be in the country with you, overseeing some of Mama's projects for the wedding."

"What, instead of dancing with all the young bucks at Almack's or riding out in the park?"

"You know I don't care much for that kind of thing, Papa. The *haut monde* is Joia's milieu, not mine."

"No, you'd rather be in the lending library or attending a dry-as-dust lecture."

"Actually," she said with a smile, easily countering his move, "I'd rather be at university, but I am resigned to my lot. I did get to visit some of the museums and such, showing Merry about, to her dismay, I might add. I'm sure she wasn't sorry to see me go. But are you sorry we were forced to come home early without Mama and the others?"

"Lud, no. One more afternoon sitting around drinking catlap with all those old biddies and I'd have driven Joia and Comfort over the border myself."

"That wouldn't be how you happened to trip over Merry's dog, would it?"

The earl studied the board more carefully. "Fool animal shouldn't have been in London in the first place."

"And you shouldn't have been feeding him scraps of bacon on the sly to keep him underfoot. But don't worry, I won't tell Mama."

"Your mother always knows everything there is to know, young lady, and it's only two weeks before she returns. We might have some company before then anyway, so we won't be rattling around by ourselves. I invited young Rendell to bring some friends for the hunting. Someone might as well be enjoying my horses while I can't."

"What, did you see Evan in London? I never did. Is he down from university, then?"

"Never saw the boy. Saw his father, though, extended the invite through him."

"I didn't know Mr. Rendell was back in this country. Evan's last letter never mentioned it."

"He is, saw him at m'club. Chap's as brown as those coffee beans he's been importing." He brushed that aside, with one of her pawns, to get to the meat of the matter. "But about Evan. Seems he and Cambridge have finally convinced Rendell that his son is no scholar, so the lad will be in Berkshire within the month."

"Then we're sure to see him, if you've offered to mount him and his friends. You know our stables are far superior to his grandfather Blakely's. Check."

"Fustian, poppet. Young Rendell always spent more time here than at his grandparents' house when he wasn't at school, and it's not because of my cattle." He studied the board a minute. "Nor because our cook is finer than Squire Blakely's, either."

Holly tried not to blush. "He's always found companionship at Winterpark. There were no children near the Manor for him to play with."

Lord Carroll snorted. "You're not children anymore, my girl." He put down the knight he was thinking of moving, to stare at his middle daughter. "Fact is, I've been thinking it's time for you and young Rendell to announce your engagement. We could do it at the Christmas ball, don't you know, and let your mother start planning for that June wedding she wants so badly."

Holly took her glasses off to polish. "Papa, you know nothing is definite between Evan and myself."

"Gammon, my dear. It's been understood between our family and the Blakelys since the two of you were in leading strings. I'm sure the servants have been making book on the match ever since your come-out."

"But Evan won't want to get married so young, Papa. You know all he wants to do is join the army."

"Which old man Blakely ain't about to permit, him with no better heir than his eldest daughter's cub. There's Rendell's fortune, too, bigger than Golden Ball's, they say, and growing faster than his shipping lines. With no entailment there either, who else will the nabob leave the whole to except his son?"

"Not that I'm wishing any ill to befall Evan, but Mr. Rendell is young enough to start another family."

"After what the Blakely chit did to him? Not likely, though he's got enough blunt for as many families as he wants. Deuce take it, poppet, why are we talking about Rendell Senior, when it's Junior who matters? Evan's father is practically in Trade. 'Sides, he'll be off on his travels again before you can say jackrabbit. It's the Blakelys who have guardianship of Evan, and Squire is as anxious as I am to see our families joined. Theirs is a fine old family in the landed gentry, and you'd be right here, near your mother."

"But Evan never wanted to be a gentleman farmer."

"Young Rendell will do what his grandfather says. Squire's had the raising of the nipper, hasn't he? Trust me, poppet, one word from you and we'll have Rendell up to scratch, I swear it."

Holly had always known this moment would be coming; she just thought she had more time. "I . . . I'm not sure that's what I want, Papa."

"What, getting missish on me, Holly? Damn, you aren't going to turn as particular as Joia, are you?"

"No, Papa."

Lord Carroll patted her hand, the chess game forgotten. "Knew you wouldn't. You're the sensible one, thank goodness. You talk to young Rendell, think about taking over at Blakely Manor. You'll have your books and your music, just what you like. You can still help your mother with the parish duties, and then there will be children of your own."

But Holly wasn't sure she wanted to be a mere chatelaine and childbearer. Papa had her best interests in mind, she didn't doubt, for hadn't he picked the right husband for Joia? Oh, Joia might have thought she'd chosen Comfort, but Holly knew better. The two were a perfect match, both beautiful, aristocratic ornaments of Polite Society. And Joia liked how Comfort was used to commanding respect and obedience. Why, her sister would have married awful Oliver if the viscount hadn't come along to deal with the midden mole. Joia needed a man like Comfort to take care of her. Holly didn't. She would have skewered the rodent with her embroidery scissors rather than let him coerce her into a marriage of dire inconvenience.

Holly didn't know about Evan. He'd always been content to let her direct their games, decide which path to ride. Did she want a biddable husband any more than she wanted one who expected her to follow his lead? Telling a female what to do was a man's right by the laws of the land. Papa seemed to think so.

"Young Rendell will make you a fine husband," he said now, sensing her doubts. "Of course, he's not up to your weight in the brain box, but most men ain't, Holly, my girl, and that's a fact. Just look at your mother and me. Bess lets me handle all the big problems, like the Regency Bill and the war with France; she handles all the rest, and we both know it."

Holly had to laugh. Papa would no more dictate to Mama than he would ride one of his prized horses into the ground.

"I know you're worried that Evan's too young, but that's just because boys mature slower than girls. Of course, you were born wise, poppet. Still, it's all to the good. This way you can mold him, train him up to be just the husband you want before he gets set in any bad habits."

Fine, Holly thought, she might as well marry Merry's dog.

Papa waited till breakfast the next morning before renewing his attack. He was reading the mail Bartholemew had brought into the morning room. "Ah, good. Rendell has accepted my invite."

"Why are you surprised, Papa? Evan has never refused a chance to make free of Winterpark's stables. If he wasn't so horse-mad, he'd never have deigned to play with three females."

"Not Evan, his father. I told you I met up with him in Town.

His business is nearly concluded, he writes, and he can join us in a sennight or so."

"Here at Winterpark? Why is that man coming to us when his own estate, Rendell Hall, and his in-laws' manor house are in the same neighborhood?"

"You have to know about the bad feeling between Rendell and the Blakelys, Holly."

"Of course, everyone in the neighborhood knows he left here a week after his wedding to Squire Blakely's daughter. Why, if the man has visited the Manor five times since, it's more than I can recall."

"And Rendell Hall hasn't been lived in since he was Evan's age, and not much then, with his own parents in India. Rendell's father made his fortune in the Trading Company, don't you know. The old man bought the Hall so Rendell, Evan's father, had somewhere to go on school holidays since there were no other relatives to claim him. Rendell Hall is shrouded in dust covers now, with the merest caretaking staff. No knowing what condition the place is in. I couldn't ask Rendell to put up there."

"But, Papa, why did you have to ask that dreadful man at all?"

"He is Evan's father, for all he aban—that is, he left the infant with his in-laws when the boy's mother died. What was he to do with a child on his travels? He was a stripling himself, with his own reasons for going off. Aye, and he multiplied his father's fortune ten times over, by all reports. They say he could have had a title any time he wanted. Maybe he'll take one now, to leave to his son."

"Evan would much rather have a brevet than a baronetcy. And if Mr. Rendell is so wealthy, he can stay in a grand hotel in London. Evan would be pleased to visit if his father deigned to ask him."

"But it's more friendly-like here in the country." The earl waited for a footman to bring a fresh pot of coffee. "Fact is, I want to convince him not to sell Rendell Hall."

"I cannot imagine why, Papa. As you say, he never uses it, nor does Evan."

"The old barn would make a dandy wedding present."

"Papa! You never discussed this with Mr. Rendell, did you? You know Evan and I haven't come to any understanding."

Lord Carroll stirred another lump of sugar into his coffee, wishing he could sweeten his daughter's tone. "Now, Holly, there's no reason to fly into the boughs. The nabob doesn't need the old barn, and you and Evan ought to have a place of your own, out from under old Mrs. Blakely's thumb. You'd have the place shipshape in no time at all, and have a grand time redecorating it, too. I daresay you'd put in an Egyptian Room and a new music room and a fancy conservatory so you can raise those plants you're always researching."

"On Mr. Rendell's money."

"You don't have to talk about him as if the chap is a solicitor or something. He's Evan's father, he ought to do right by the boy."

Holly was indignant on her old playmate's behalf. "What kind of father never sees his son?"

The spoon clattered against the earl's cup as he reflected on another boy, another father. "One with circumstances beyond his control, by Jupiter. And Evan never wanted for anything, missy."

"Anything but a father."

That hurt. "You don't know what happened, you don't know what he did for the boy, how hard I— Confound it, you get more like your mother every day."

"Thank you, Papa."

He had to smile at that. "I meant no compliment then, and well you know it. Your mother can be the stubbornest woman on earth. At least you don't hold young Rendell's parentage against him. I wish you'd consider the match, Holly, for I've a yearning to see my girls settled before I'm too old to walk them down the aisle. Give the boy a chance, for me."

Chapter Thirteen

*L*ady Carroll returned from London sooner than expected. Joia's trousseau wasn't complete; they hadn't found just the right shade of blue for the new dining room seat covers; the invitations had not been delivered from the printers. But come home, Lady Carroll would, to give her husband a piece of her mind.

"How could you invite the nabob here, Bradford, without telling me we were going to be entertaining one of the wealthiest men in the country?"

Lord Carroll looked around for Bartholemew, the obvious informant. For once, the traitor was playing least in sight. "He's only a man, Bess. Not even a nobleman."

"So? Were you going to bed him down with the grooms and offer him bachelor fare? Cold meats and free run of your stables?"

"Of course not, Bess. I—"

The countess was not going to give him a chance. "Furthermore, Bradford, your wits must have gone begging, to invite Evan and his rackety friends to stop here when you know Holly is the only female in the house, unchaperoned at that. What could you have been thinking?"

He'd been thinking that he'd get the deed done before his beloved wife put a crimp in his plans to see Holly settled, and settled well, by George, before the New Year. "I missed you, Bess."

Truth to tell, Lady Carroll didn't have to return so hastily from the metropolis. Bartholemew would have made sure the merchant prince was treated royally: his rooms heated for one more used to warmer climates, the menus enlarged from Bradford's preferred simple country fare. And Hollice never got flustered. At nineteen she was poised enough to act the hostess, Bess thought with pride, even for a world traveler. Hollice was such a sensible girl, the countess could also have trusted her to keep Evan and his friends from crossing the line. Meredyth would have been in their midst, up to every rig and row, and Joia . . . well, Lady Carroll was beginning to see the wisdom of an early wedding as far as Joia and her onetime rake were concerned. But trustworthy Hollice was the comfortable one, the practical daughter who thought everything out before she acted. Now Bess was going to make sure her middle child wasn't talked into a practical, comfortable match. A good marriage wasn't based on any intellectual principles of logic—or any impatient father's scheming. "I missed you, too, dear."

Evan and his friends arrived in a whirlwind just at dinnertime, filling Winterpark's entry hall with uniforms, greatcoats, servants, baggage, and noise. Merry's dog was ecstatic at having so many strangers to greet, barking and leaping and tearing from one laughing young man to the other. In her efforts to capture the animal before Downsy toppled one of the unwary guests, Holly noticed a dark-skinned, older gentleman in the shadows. This had to be Evan's father, the missing Midas.

Mr. Rendell was heavily muffled and seemed reluctant to part with his wraps when Bartholemew would have relieved him. When he did take off his hat, Holly could see that he had brown hair, darker than Evan's, but with blond streaks through it from the sun. Next to his tanned complexion, the effect was exotic but not unattractive, Holly had to admit. He was fit, she could tell from his well-tailored clothes, and pleasantly featured. Mr. Rendell wasn't as devastatingly handsome as Joia's viscount, but neither was he as old, harsh, and weathered as she'd expected from Evan's descriptions. The man wasn't an ogre, after all. Not in looks, at any rate.

Then it was time for greetings and introductions. Evan correctly bowed to Holly's mother and shook the earl's hand before reverting to the Evan they all knew by bussing Joia on the cheek. "You should have waited for me, you heartless wench," he teased. Next he swung Merry off her feet in a wide circle, her skirts and petticoats flying. "Merry-berry, what a beauty you're turning out to be! No more runny nose either," he noted, which, of course, had Merry with her red hair and fair complexion turning every shade of crimson. Then Evan pretended to search the entryway until his eyes alit on Holly. "Why, I hardly recognized you, Hol, without the glasses and braids. There's my girl." And he enveloped her in a hug that was more suffocating than anything else. Holly feared the rose at her neckline was sadly crushed, and she knew her hair, so carefully pinned atop her head, was falling about her shoulders. She should have kept the braids, knowing Evan was coming.

He was making the rest of the introductions, the earl and countess passing the young men down the informal receiving line to their daughters and Comfort, who had, naturally, followed Joia to the country. Mr. Rendell bowed politely when it was his turn and said a few words to everyone, Holly noted, but without Evan's high spirits or ready grin. He did bow over her hand, singling her out, calling her Lady Hollice, so she knew Papa had spoken to him. Holly stiffened her spine and stood a bit taller. If the man was here on an inspection tour, too bad. She was Evan's friend, crushed flower and all, not his.

After everyone was made known to one another, the gathering adjourned to the drawing room, except for Holly, who had to repair her hair. When she returned, Evan and some of his friends were interrogating Lord Comfort and Papa about the latest war news from London. A handful of others were flirting with Joia, engagement ring or not, and two young officers in Horse Guards uniform were asking Merry about the hunt and the horses. Mr. Rendell stood aside, stroking the ears of Merry's dog, who was quiet for once, exhausted by the commotion. Before Holly could seek out one sister or the other, Bartholemew announced dinner.

Comfort escorted Joia to the dining room, and Evan went right along with them, pursuing his conversation with the viscount, followed by his other military-minded friends. Merry was between her two soldiers, leaving Holly to fend for herself.

Really, Holly thought, Evan should have made sure she was escorted. His father seemed to agree, for Mr. Rendell bowed before her and silently offered his arm. "Unmannered pup," he muttered. She didn't think he meant Merry's dog.

Evan was seated next to her, but he might have been at the opposite end of the table for all the conversation they had. With so few ladies present, talk was general, loud, and devoted almost entirely to equestrian pursuits. Mr. Rendell, Holly noted, seated next to Mama, added little to the cheerful hum. Evan obviously inherited his love of horses from his mother's side of the family, as well as his outgoing nature. Perhaps Mr. Rendell had done him a favor after all, she considered, leaving Evan to be raised by the Blakelys. A father cold enough to walk away from his own motherless son wouldn't be much of a parent.

During the last course, Evan told Holly that they had to talk later, he had great news to tell her. She wasn't surprised when he came to sit beside her at the pianoforte after dinner, but she was startled when her mother suggested Holly take Evan to see the new family portrait hanging in the library. Evan didn't care about art; the countess did care about the conventions. Therefore, Holly concluded, Mama must also favor the match.

Lady Carroll watched her middle daughter go off with her old playmate, certain that a few minutes spent alone with the likable, light-minded Evan would convince Hollice they wouldn't suit.

Evan didn't bother looking at the portrait over the mantel. He grabbed one of Holly's hands and tugged her to the sofa, where he sat sideways, facing her. "Capital news, Hol. M'father says he'll purchase my colors as soon as I've got an heir. So what do you say we get buckled, old girl?"

Holly could see herself, frail and bent, with a sweet little girl at her knees asking, "How did Grandfather propose, Grandma?" And she'd have to repeat: " 'So what do you say we get buckled, old girl?' "

She didn't know whether to laugh or to cry, so she stalled. "Why can't your father get his own successor after you? He's certainly young enough, much younger than I expected. I daresay he's no older than my mother."

"He's six and thirty, and he doesn't care about that flummery of an heir and a spare. It's Grandfather Blakely who won't have any closer kin to take over if I cash in my chips, which I don't intend to do anytime soon. The old boy is set on having his way, though, so this is the best I can manage. What do you think?"

"About your signing up? I hate it, Evan. Bullets and cannon-balls don't care about your intentions to live forever."

"No, goose, about us getting legshackled. M'father says we can have Rendell Hall. I know how you like managing things, so that should please you. Or else you could live with m'grand-parents. They could use some help now that they're getting on."

They'd been getting on since Holly was a child. Now they were getting curmudgeonly. "Evan, are you telling me that I have my choice of residing at Rendell Hall or Blakely Manor after we're wed, while you are off with the army?"

"I didn't suppose you'd want to stay on here with your parents, but if that's what'll make you happy, Holly, I'm sure your father won't mind, the way he dotes on you girls."

"You don't think I ought to be with my husband?"

"What, at the front? That's no place for a lady, Holly. I'd be a hundred kinds of cad to drag you off to live in a tent and cook your own supper and wash your clothes in a stream." He waved his hand around at the luxury of Winterpark. "After this? Don't be a hen-wit, Holly. Think of the child."

And don't think of having an adventure of your own, she extrapolated from his words, *just stay all cozy and safe, breeding Berkshire Blakelys, raising rural Rendells.* While her husband was off getting killed.

Evan could sense her lack of enthusiasm for the plan, perhaps by the way she was tapping her foot and shaking her head. "It won't be for long, Holly. I'll be back soon and we can go to London, do the sights and all. Or Bath. But if I don't get to go now, Boney'll be defeated and I'll never see action. M'father's sure the end is in sight, and he has more sources for information than the War Office does. He's going off to Austria soon, but he says he'll make the arrangements for me to join a crack cavalry unit as soon as you give the nod."

"Evan, I don't think . . ."

He jumped up and started pacing back and forth in front of the fireplace. "Dash it, Holly, don't be getting all missish on me. I counted on your understanding because you know better than anyone how I've always wanted to sign up. Now I can, if you'll agree to get hitched. I even brought a special license with me so we can get started on that nursery sooner." He took an official-looking document out of his pocket and spread it on the striped cushion next to her. "This didn't come cheap, old girl. I had to ask m'father to advance this quarter's allowance for it. He was decent about that, too."

"I thought you hated the man you used to call sir. Now it's m'father this and m'father that. What happened to the resentment you harbored against him all your life for deserting you? Is he less cold and unfeeling now that he's offered to purchase your colors?" She couldn't keep the bitterness out of her voice. If Mr. Rendell hadn't suddenly imposed himself on their lives, at this late date, they wouldn't be having this conversation.

Evan smoothed out the license so she wouldn't see his blush. "He kept me on tight purse strings, was all. I shouldn't have complained to you, I guess. With all his blunt, I figured m'father could afford better horses for me and a place of my own in Town. I was aggravated when he wouldn't spring for a high-perch phaeton last year either."

"The man has some sense, then. I've seen how you drive."

"I could still teach you a thing or two, missy. Who was it tipped your father's curricle in the ditch that time?"

"You distracted me."

As she was distracting him now. Holly was happier that their relationship was back to its usual footing, but Evan wasn't letting their familiar bickering stop him from showing his sire in a better light. When Holly took a dislike to someone, she never let up, which would be deuced awkward in a daughter-in-law.

Running anxious fingers through his sandy hair, Evan said, "Dash it, Hol, that ain't the point. M'father's top of the trees, b'gad, and I'm sorry I gave you the wrong impression of him. Of course, I used to resent not going along on his jaunts, but a chap don't take an infant to China, does he? He did write regularly from wherever he happened to be, and sent gifts from every port. Whenever he was in the country he visited me at school, on account of not being comfortable at Squire's. Which ain't to say he didn't come down heavy to keep the place in repair. The manor would have crumbled into compost if m'father hadn't spent his brass on it. And he had no reason to be so generous, not after what the Blakelys did to him."

"What exactly did they do?" Holly wanted to know, and not just to delay giving her old friend an answer. She'd been curious about the Rendells forever, it seemed. "No one would ever say."

Evan was pacing again. "I never had the straight of it myself. Couldn't very well ask m'grandfather, could I? Or ask m'father in a letter. Bad form, that. Shouldn't even be discussing it out of the family, but if you're going to be part of it, you have a right to know. And I trust you, naturally. Fact is, the servants knew as much as anyone, so I got to hear how there was a ball at the Manor, and how m'father was invited over from Rendell Hall. He and m'mother were discovered in the summerhouse. They were sleeping all innocent-like, but the damage was done. M'father swore his wine had been drugged, but he still had to do the honorable thing."

98

"Your mother entrapped him?"

Evan shrugged. "She might have been drugged, too, no one knows. Thing is, the manor house was falling down around Squire's ears and he had four daughters with no dowries. The Rendells were wealthy. Not as deep-pocketed as now, but more than enough for Squire's needs. M'father should have been downier, but he wasn't more than eighteen. I suppose *his* parents shouldn't have sent him to England on his own, but they wanted him to be a proper English gentleman."

"So he ended up with a not-quite-proper English wife."

He nodded. "Then I came along. Thing is, he'd grown suspicious fast, and wondered if I was part of the reason for the trap, to give Blakely's daughter a name for her, ah, indiscretion. When she died he washed his hands of the whole family and went off to make his own fortune."

"But what about you? Didn't he care that you were alone with those awful, deceitful people?" She'd never liked Squire Blakely. Now she knew why.

"Don't be a gudgeon, Holly. He didn't think I was his."

"That's nonsense. Anyone can see the resemblance about your eyes, and the shape of your head is the same."

"Yes, but no one could see it in a hairless, mewling infant, so he left. He didn't renege on his responsibilities the way another man might have, thinking he'd been compromised and cuckolded. I understand all that now, Holly. And truly, it didn't hurt me any."

But Holly knew it had, knew how the lonely little boy had envied her for her own father. And now he wanted to do the same to his son, to Holly's son. He wanted to conceive a child only to leave him to go fight a war.

"So what do you say, old girl? You know your father and mother approve. They'd have sent old Barty in here ages ago otherwise. Should we shake on it?"

Shake on it? This was the only marriage proposal Holly might ever get—especially if she accepted it—and he wanted to shake hands. Shouldn't marriage involve something more? she wondered. "I don't know, Evan. We've been friends for so long, but marriage is different. I need to think about it."

"Dash it, Holly, what have you been thinking about for the last nineteen years?"

That was a good question, too.

Chapter Fourteen

*H*olly wanted romance.

Joia was the fairy princess and Merry was the madcap. Holly was supposed to be the daughter with her feet on the ground, the reliable one. But she read, she listened, she observed—and she knew there was a world apart from her own universe. She imagined, too, all the different sights and smells, the new languages to be learned, the strange customs to be observed besides the proper depth of a curtsy at Almack's. Holly wanted to live, before she lived the rest of her placid, reliable life.

She stayed on in the library, smoothing the edges of the special license Evan had left behind. That was also typical of Evan, she thought, carelessly misplacing such an important prize. He knew she'd look after it for him as always, even if the scrap of paper was her death sentence, just as he expected her to look after his home and his son. Evan would have his Grand Adventure. Holly would have his grandparents.

Everyone seemed to want Holly to say yes, to get the deed done so they could move on with their own lives. Merry thought the uniforms were dashing; an officer for a brother-in-law would suit her to the ground. Mama would like to see her settled nearby. And Papa, well, Papa seemed to have sensed his own mortality all of a sudden. That folderol with Oliver had sorely affected him. Holly wondered if the earl had some scheme afoot to replace Oliver in the succession with his first grandson, the way he was so eager to get her and Joia fired off. Lud, what a coil that would be! He'd have to petition the courts and the College of Records, possibly Parliament. And he'd have to have Oliver declared incompetent to take over the earldom, which he was, of course, but no more so than half the members of Parliament who would be voting. Mama would hate the scandalbroth being stirred that way.

And Evan wanted Holly to agree to the marriage. He was such a good friend that she wanted to see him happy, and knew she could do it, first by standing up with him, then by standing aside while he pursued his dream. Later he'd be content with his fields and his horses, with the occasional jaunt to London, where he wouldn't want to attend lectures, musicales, or museums. Would that make her content? Holly wondered.

As she made her way back to the drawing room, she passed Bartholemew in the hall, directing the footmen who were wheeling in the tea cart. The butler gave her a sharp look, then nodded to himself as if his question had been answered.

"What are the odds, Barty?" she asked softly, outside the door.

Bartholemew didn't pretend to misunderstand. "They were dead even, Lady Holly, but now it's more of a pool. Not a matter of whether, but when."

"I see," she said, feeling another door close as she stepped into the drawing room ahead of the servants.

She didn't hear Bartholemew mutter to himself: "When hell freezes over ought to be the safest bet."

Lord and Lady Carroll were sitting to one end of the double-square parlor with the Blakelys, who'd driven over after dinner to see Evan. Joia and the viscount were in the corner, in their own private world. At the other end of the room, Merry had organized Evan and his friends into two teams for a game of charades that was getting more uproarious with every missed clue. Mr. Rendell sat by himself near the windows, a book in his hands, a still, dark presence, neither seeking company nor inviting it.

Half the heads in the room swiveled in her direction, looking for the answer to the question they all knew had been asked.

Holly made her mouth curve into a noncommittal smile as she stepped farther into the room, her slippers making no sound on the thick carpet. The conversations and contest resumed.

Holly should have joined the youngest members of the gathering at their game. Merry shouldn't have been alone in the center of a handful of carefree youths who, unless Holly missed her guess, had sampled too liberally of her father's port after dinner. Instead she retreated to her own sanctuary, the pianoforte along the far wall.

Holly lost herself in the music, where she didn't have to think, until a soft voice beside her said, "You play very well. I thought the whelp was boasting of some schoolgirlish talent when he said you could play. I see that he spoke the truth."

Mr. Rendell was there, with a cup of tea for her. Holly nodded her thanks, and when he seemed to be expecting more, she added, "I am surprised Evan mentioned a thing like that. He isn't very musical himself, you know."

Still standing—Holly hadn't invited him to join her on the bench—Rendell glanced over to the rowdy bunch still involved in their game. "He's just a pup. He'll grow up."

Which was just what her father had said. But Evan wouldn't grow up, not if he became cannon fodder. "He respects you," Holly said. "Why don't you take him in hand?"

Mr. Rendell still watched Evan acting out some nonsense while his friends hooted at him. "I believe I gave up that right."

Holly stood, leaving her cup on the bench beside her. "And I do not believe I want the responsibility." She turned to leave, but felt a touch on her arm.

"Wait, please. Lady Hollice, you don't seem to like me. I would know why."

She looked at the gloved hand on her elbow, wondering if it was as brown as the man's face. "I do not know you, sir, so I would not presume to pass judgment. I do not, however, like the way you raised your son."

His brows rose and he turned his head to the side, a gesture Evan had always employed. "But, Lady Hollice, I did not raise Evan."

"Exactly." She dipped the shallowest of curtsies. "Pray excuse me, my mother needs help with the tea things."

The following day Evan took his friends out with Lord Carroll's hunters and hounds, but not with his daughters. The lads rode too hard, the earl decreed, with a look to Evan that warned of dire consequences should one of the horses arrive home lame. They were all like-minded sportsmen, though, to whom fine horseflesh was more important than their own necks.

Merry was sulking in the barn with her dog because she couldn't ride along; Joia and Mama were working on the wedding invitations lists; and the earl and his prospective son-in-law were at the solicitor's office in Carrolton, finalizing the marriage settlement documents.

Holly couldn't concentrate on her music, her drawing, or her attempts to learn German from the guidebook Joia had purchased, then discarded. She decided to poke through the library, to see if anything there could hold her interest.

The last thing she wanted was another conversation with Evan's father. She hastily backed toward the door when she saw him sitting at one of the desks, papers spread around him. His neckcloth was loosened and his sun-streaked hair, longer than the current fashion, had come loose of its queue.

He looked up at the sound, quickly stood, and said, "Please don't go."

"No, I am sorry for disturbing you." She was half out the door.

"Please, Lady Hollice, you would be doing me a favor. I have been at this all morning and could use a respite." He waved an ink-stained hand at the papers on the desk.

"I'll . . . I'll have Bartholemew bring in a tea tray, sir."

"But you won't stay?" He didn't wait for an answer, but walked toward her and the exit. "Then let me be the one to leave. This is your house and I do not wish to displace you, especially from such a magnificent library. I only wish I had time to explore the shelves myself. I see some familiar friends, and some interesting titles that haven't come my way."

A compliment to the library was one of the quickest ways to win Holly's rare smile. "It is a wonderful place, isn't it? But please, sir, I am being impolite. We can share the library." She gestured Rendell back to the desk, but he grimaced.

"No, I need a rest. I have a report from one of my shipping companies, but I swear the fellow writing the accounting never learned to hold a pen. I cannot tell if he's trying to hide irregularities, or trying to hide the fact that he cannot spell. Deuce take it if I can make heads or tails of the clunch's hen-scratches."

"Would you like me to try? I've been deciphering Papa's scrawls for years."

"Would you? And yes, I think I need some tea. You will need sustenance, too, after you see what the paperskull's done to the King's English."

Holly took the spectacles out of her pocket. What could her looks matter here? Mr. Rendell stared at her in his quietly appraising way, not precisely discourteous, but disconcerting. Then he nodded and pulled glasses out of his own pocket. "See here, this line?" he pointed out without further comment. "Either I had three ships sink, or I purchased thirty-two bottles of ink."

Holly was able to help Evan's father decipher most of the blotches, and devour most of a tray of Cook's fresh scones. She'd found the report fascinating, so was able to tell him in all honesty that his thank-yous were unnecessary, that she'd been happy to help.

"But I would have had to send the thing back to my secretaries in London, then wait for its return. Surely there must be some way I can show my gratitude, Lady Hollice."

"First, you can start calling me Holly. Only Mama uses my real name."

"If you will call me Ren. *No one* calls me by my real name, Hammond, thank goodness, for they'd shorten it to Ham, and your 'Mr. Rendell' makes me feel ancient. What is second?"

"Do you speak German? I am trying to learn, and I understand you are going to Austria on business."

"I do. I'd be useless to my enterprises there, otherwise. I find it absurd how many of our countrymen feel that it's the world's duty to learn English. I would be happy to help you with your pronunciation, if that's what's bothering you, on the condition that I can call on your assistance again if I hear from this cretin in Cairo."

"That would be my pleasure." Holly thought she really would enjoy learning more about business matters.

"Excellent. Shall we say tomorrow at this time?"

"Do you not intend to ride tomorrow? Papa would be happy to lend you a mount."

"If by riding you mean the neck-or-nothing, cross-country free-for-alls, no, I leave that sport to Evan and his friends. But a pleasant ride in the country sounds appealing if the weather holds. Perhaps you and Evan would accompany me tomorrow afternoon to Rendell Hall. We should be coming to a decision about its future."

Holly's future, he meant. She swallowed. "I'm sure that's for you and Evan to consider, sir."

Ren raised one eloquent eyebrow, but he didn't say anything. Unlike Papa, this man hid his thoughts and his emotions. He was not, at least, pushing Holly into accepting Evan. Reassured by that, she felt comfortable enough with him to ask, "Why did you finally relent and give your permission for Evan to join the army? You cannot wish your only child to go off to war."

"Hardly. I have seen enough conflicts throughout the world to know that wars are won by wealthy old men; they are lost by poor young ones. But it was his fondest wish." Ren didn't say that he found it hard to deny Evan, that a guilty heart was in conflict with a wiser head. "I felt I had to give my consent, but I didn't make it easy for him."

"No, you've made it harder for me," Holly objected. "If I wed Evan, he's thrown into danger. If I don't, he's thwarted in his ambition. I don't want to hold anyone's life in my hands that way."

"I'm sorry, Holly, I never thought of your place in this. In truth, I thought my terms would keep him out of the army. I believed he'd be like other young men, too loath to give up his freedom to exchange it for an officer's uniform. I assumed the idea of parson's mousetrap would have him hying back to school in a wink. I hadn't counted on his great affection for you. Then I hoped that a wife might set his mind to other avenues than war, but as you say, that would cost his dreams. I . . . I do not know him well enough."

Holly heard so much regret in Ren's voice that she told him, "He doesn't hold that against you, you know."

But she did, and he blamed himself. Deuce take it, Ren thought, how could he know what was best for his son when years went by without his remembering he *had* a son? Now this lovely young woman was caught in the same snare.

"What do you think he will do," she was asking, "if I don't marry him?"

"You mean do I think he'll find some Covent Garden doxy to wed? No, I was clever enough to stipulate he had to make an acceptable marriage. And I don't think even he is army-mad enough to take the King's shilling. I had hoped to offer him a position at one of my businesses, to see if he'd be interested enough to stay."

The idea of Evan in business, sitting behind a desk, made Holly chuckle. "He'll never sit still long enough. Besides, if you think your Cairo correspondent has poor penmanship, you should see Evan's."

"I have and you're right. I'd have to hire the bantling a secretary of his own. Then, too, the single-minded brat would only save his wages to buy a commission. Or else he'll do it when he comes into Squire's property. Blakely can't live forever, and it's the old man who's insisting on an heir, not myself."

"So he'll go off to war sooner or later, no matter what we do?"

"We could pray that Bonaparte is defeated tomorrow, but that's not likely. And there is always a war going on somewhere for valiant fools to fight." He put his spectacles back in his pocket and sighed. "At least the army will make a man out of him. Nothing ages a lad quicker than his first battle. Maybe he'll have his fill of adventure then, and be ready to come home and settle down."

"You never did."

Ren looked at her, his head to one side. "I never had a reason to."

Chapter Fifteen

*F*lowers and fields thrived in the rain. Gatherings of restless young men did not. When a storm arrived, bringing winds that felled trees and downpours that flooded roads, the mostly male house party started to decamp. Without the hunting, they may as well be back in London where they could visit the clubs and ogle the opera dancers. Evan was left with no like-minded company and no occupation. He did visit his grandparents and he did practice his billiards, but mostly he followed Holly around, expecting her to devise entertainment for them as she always did.

Her parents' plan to throw them together was working. She seethed. Evan was growing on her—like mildew. Holly would rather be working on her German or helping Mr. Rendell with his papers. His handwriting turned out to be nearly as hopeless as Evan's, so she offered to write some of his letters, meanwhile listening to Ren's ideas, stories of his travels, the plans he was making for new ventures.

Instead of being so pleasantly engaged, Holly was forced to spend hours amusing a guest who did not like books or music, who did not like losing whether they played cards or the old nursery games, and who wanted to reenact for her edification every battle of the Peninsular campaign.

"It's not polite to leave your father alone so often, Evan. Papa's gout is bothering him too much to be good company, and everyone else is too involved with wedding plans, with the date barely five weeks away. Comfort's parents will both be coming, so Mama is in a fidge over how to keep them separated. Your father has no one for conversation."

"I'm glad you're taking to him, Hol. I told you the pater was great guns, didn't I? Did I explain Wellesley's strategies for the stand at Coruña?"

Comfort took pity on Holly one afternoon when it seemed as if rain had been falling for weeks instead of days. Reluctantly leaving Joia's side—she was busy with the local seamstress—the viscount invited Evan to practice fencing with him, since they were both needing the exercise.

They took over the ballroom, after promising Lady Carroll to keep clear of the gold velvet draperies, the striped silk wallpaper, and the newly re-covered chairs. Evan was content for two blessed afternoons, during which Holly learned six irregular verbs, the proper way to address a Bedouin chief, and a new Beethoven sonata. Along with his correspondence, Mr. Rendell'd had his London couriers bring the music and some books he thought might interest Holly. His messengers had no trouble getting through the mired roads; at the prices the nabob was paying, they would have swum.

On the third afternoon Evan had the knacky notion to invite Holly to watch, thinking to impress her with his prowess. "And you too, sir," he said, inviting his father. "You must be dashed sick of this musty library and your dry-as-dust papers."

Merry and Joia came along, and the earl and countess, too, for a diversion. Half the servants also seemed to be in the ballroom, making book, no one doubted.

The foils, of course, were buttoned.

Comfort and Evan were evenly matched. The viscount had ten years' more experience, but Evan had youthful stamina and a wiry athleticism that Comfort's larger, more muscular frame could not duplicate. They wore slippers, breeches, and shirtsleeves, and Holly couldn't help noticing Joia's avid interest in Comfort's undress. As for herself, she was interested in getting back to Mr. Rendell's theories concerning the future of steam locomotion. Then he quietly asked if he might challenge the winner of the match.

Comfort bowed politely and waited for Evan to help Mr. Rendell shrug himself out of his superfine coat and his shoes.

When he removed his neckcloth and unbuttoned the collar of his shirt so he had more freedom of movement, Holly began to understand Joia's fascination. Who would have thought the male figure could be so attractive?

Evan was frowning. "I say, sir, don't you think you ought to wear a face mask?" Even Lady Carroll appeared worried, for scarring the wealthiest man in England would be decidedly bad ton.

"I don't think that will be necessary, bantling."

And it wasn't, not by half. Rendell wasn't more experienced or more agile; he was, quite simply, a master. The most novice of watchers could recognize at a glance that Comfort was literally defenseless against the older man's blade, when they could see the flashing steel at all.

The viscount stepped back and held up his hand in surrender. "I have been gulled, I believe," he said with a smile. "The only way I'll take you on again, sir, is if you use your left hand."

Ren cocked his head to the side, then he tossed his sword in the air. Without a glance from Rendell, it arced, flickered, and landed in his other hand. "But, my lord, I am left-handed."

Evan's mouth was hanging open. Holly feared hers was, too. The earl was laughing and slapping his thigh. "Deuced good show, Rendell. Where did you learn such skill?"

"Here and there," was all he said, gesturing Evan to take his place. "Come, twig. If you want to be a soldier, you must sharpen your techniques." Everyone could see he was going easy on Evan, moving more slowly, letting the younger man set the pace and take the offensive. Still, in five minutes Evan was wiping sweat from his eyes and breathing through his mouth. Rendell was chatting as if he were at tea. "The English, you see, are too predictable. I can recognize an Italian instructor in your stance, while Lord Comfort studied with a Frenchman. Northern France, I'd hazard. The French have finesse, the Italians have the speed, the Spanish, where the swords of fables were born, have the flair. Russians and Slavs depend more on strength, the Orientals more on control. You must learn them all, brat, before you take on the world."

"What . . . do . . . Englishmen have?" Evan panted.

"Perseverance, halfling, bloody single-minded persever-ance, no matter how poor the odds or how lost the cause. An Englishman doesn't give up."

So Evan asked Holly again when they finally got the chance to ride out to Rendell Hall, two days later. "This shilly-shallying ain't like you, Hol. You always know your own mind. So what's it to be?"

"I'm sorry, Evan, I just need more time." Holly could not have said whether she needed more time to decide, or more time before taking on the role of a soldier's grass widow, Squire's brood mare. Evan was scowling, so she added, "Let's just look at the house today."

Annoyed at not getting his way, Evan rode ahead to where Merry and his father were debating the merits of purebred dogs versus mixed breeds. He rudely interrupted. "C'mon, Merry, let's race."

Mr. Rendell smiled at Merry and nodded, then let his horse fall back until he was alongside Holly. Without commenting on her stony-faced expression or her swain's defection, Ren started giving the German name to birds, trees, and other objects as they passed them. When he couldn't think of the German, or didn't know it, he made up an absurdly long word like *hoffenschnitzel*, just to see her smile.

The two-hour ride seemed like minutes before they arrived at Rendell Hall, a sprawling Gothic edifice. "My father had an agent purchase it for him," Ren explained in excuse for the tur-rets and arched windows. "Sight unseen."

"I'll bet it's haunted." Merry was delighted at the idea. "Let's go see, Evan."

The two went exploring upstairs, arguing over the existence of ghosts, while Mr. Rendell conferred with the caretaker and his wife. Holly glanced through half-open doors at shrouded rooms, rows of armor, and hearths that could have roasted oxen, though she doubted they would warm the vast, three-storied rooms. The house didn't look haunted. It only needed people and attention, the windows widened to let in more sun; lighter, brighter hangings on the dark wood panels; children to play in the long corridors.

"How could you think of selling such a fairy-tale castle?" she asked Rendell when he rejoined her. "Don't you want to have a place of your own to come home to between travels? Don't you miss having roots someplace?"

"How can I miss what I never had? I was raised by amahs, servants, tutors, schoolmasters, in as many different houses. My roots are in the counting house."

How different her own childhood had been, Holly thought, surrounded by family, immured in the stronghold of generations of Carrolls. On the other hand, she'd never been farther than London and Bath, except for one horrendous visit to Aunt Irmentrude in Wales. "I think you can regret not having what others enjoy, what might give you pleasure."

Ren purposely misunderstood. "I have always found hotels adequate, the finest ones, of course. The chimneys in this monstrosity smoke and the windows let in drafts. I'd never patronize such an inn."

"But it's your home, or could be. You could make it perfect, I'm sure."

"It's too big, too empty for one man. He'd feel haunted indeed, if only by his own past, his own future."

"You are right. It needs a family."

He looked at her sharply, but Holly was lost in her own dreams. "I cannot think of anything better, a magic carpet to travel the world, and a magical palace to return to. I'd fill Rendell Hall with treasures from around the globe and children to enjoy them, yes, even if I had to borrow my sisters' children or the neighbors'." She twirled around, setting dust motes to dancing in the air.

"Why would you have to borrow someone else's brats?"

"Oh, if I were a man—a rich one, of course—I'd be too busy

to find a wife. Isn't that what happened to you?" she asked abruptly.

"I had a wife."

"For less than a year. Why didn't you remarry?"

How could he tell this idealistic, innocent woman-child that he could never trust another woman after Blakely's chit? That his fortune was a magnet for every adventuress in every country he'd visited. That he would rather spend the rest of his days alone in hotels than be someone else's pawn. "I was too old."

"What a taradiddle! You're not old even now. I've seen you fence, remember."

Merry and Evan came downstairs then, quibbling over the number of rooms they'd counted. Ren nodded in their direction. "All that energy makes me want to take a nap. Come, children, we have seen enough."

Holly didn't think he looked the least bit tired, sitting effortlessly atop his horse, muscles visibly working under the tautly stretched breeches. And she definitely wasn't tired of looking at Ren, so she was more curt with Evan than usual when he took the place next to her for the ride home.

"So what do you think of the house, Holly? I know you already like m'father, so that's aces. We could talk to him tonight about giving us the old pile if you want it."

"It's his house, Evan. He should keep it and make himself a home."

"Then where will you— Where will we live?"

"I had thought," she snapped at him, "to live with my husband, wherever he happened to be. I had thought my husband would want me at his side, wherever he happened to be."

"Deuce take it, Holly, we've been through that. What, do you want me to pour the butterboat over you and swear my heart will break for every minute we're apart? Is that what you want, Holly? I never took you for one of those spoiled belles, but, Zeus, I'll write you a blasted poem as soon as we're married."

Now, there was an offer, Holly thought. Not only would she be left to molder along with Rendell Hall, but she'd have to

114

read bad poetry to boot! She kicked her horse into a canter and rode alongside Merry.

When they reached Winterpark, Merry's mongrel pup caught sight of his mistress and came running to greet her, barking and tearing across the lawns. Evan's horse took exception and reared. If Evan had been paying attention, no harm would have been done. Master Rendell, however, was still in a sulk over his old friend's intransigence, insensitivity to his needs, and increasingly feminine behavior. In two shakes he was in the dirt.

Flat on his back with the wind knocked out of him, Evan still managed to hold the reins. That would have been the right thing to do, if the horse weren't still dancing around, doing crow-hops perilously close to Evan's head. The groom came running, Merry shouted for the dog, and Holly started to edge her horse between Evan and his mount—but Ren was there, leaping off his horse and over Evan's, throwing his body over his son's and rolling him out of danger.

When the dust settled, Evan was mortified. Not only had he parted company with his horse, but he'd done it in front of the girl he wanted to impress, the father who never seemed to put a foot wrong, and the brat who owned the misbegotten mutt. Since he couldn't take his frustrations out on Holly or Rendell, he shouted at Merry.

"Of all the cursed canines, that's the most miserably behaved animal I've ever seen, missy. It ought to be taken out and shot. Or you should, for your hoydenish behavior. When are you going to grow up and stop embarrassing your family?"

The front door was open—the odds-makers were working overtime—and Merry's lip was trembling, but Evan was too agitated to notice. "I was ashamed in front of my friends when they saw you in breeches in the barn. You're nothing but a draggle-tailed tomboy."

Merry was crying in Holly's arms. No one had ever yelled at her but Papa, and he never meant it.

"Hush, dearest," Holly was saying, "you did nothing wrong." To Evan, in quite a different tone of voice, she said, "I think you owe Merry an apology. Your fall was your own fault, not hers. We all saw Downsy coming across the lawn, but you weren't paying attention."

"By all that's holy, you're defending *her*? Whatever happened to loyalty?"

"She's my sister."

"And I'm the man who—"

"Has been my friend for a lifetime. Do not ruin that friendship by insulting my sister, whose manners are everything pleasing."

"Oh, yes? How pleased are you to know I caught her playing billiards with Comfort! No lady would ever do such a thing."

Holly vowed to learn that very day. Out loud she said, "The viscount obviously didn't find anything wrong with Merry's playing, so why should you, unless she beat you at that, too?"

"Now Joia's toff is the social arbiter? My opinion doesn't matter because I have no title? Is that what you're holding out for, Holly? If you are, speak to him"—jerking his head to where his father was soothing the horses—"since you're already as close as inkle-weavers. I'm sure he'll buy you a title, too. Of course, you might have to wait a few years for me to inherit it, but hell, I've been waiting a few years to join the blasted army."

Chapter Sixteen

"*I* said perseverance, twig, not persecution." The Rendells were in the ballroom, fencing. That is, one was fencing. The other was working off all his anger and frustrations on empty air, which was all Ren would let the lad hit, in such a temper. If ever there was a hotspur ready for the army, he thought, Evan was it. Too bad Blakely insisted on an heir or Ren would have the youngster shipped out tomorrow, into a safe regiment, out of action, where he knew the commanders. There would be no more of this nonsense of marrying him off to a close but incompatible match. Still, he'd vowed to keep mumchance, to let this stranger with his name make his own choices. "Gravely offending the woman one wishes to wed is bad strategy, brat."

Evan was panting, but he did manage to gasp, "The old girl's a Trojan. She never takes a pet for long. I'll have to apologize to the infant, but Holly will come around. I just wish she weren't taking so blasted long about it. I could have been with the chaps in London."

"Spoken like a true love-struck suitor. Did you ever think that you and Lady Holly mightn't suit? That she might expect more out of a marriage?"

Evan had called halt to wipe the perspiration out of his eyes. He took the conversation as an excuse to catch his wind, rather than having his father notice his labored breathing. "Like what? It ain't as if Holly's a Diamond like Joia. She don't even

117

enjoy the social whirl. Said so herself many a time. She's a regular bluestocking, in fact. Turns most fellows off, don't you know."

Ren was convinced the boy was deaf, dumb, and blind, besides being weak in the chest. "So you're actually doing her a favor by taking her off the Marriage Mart?"

Evan tipped his head in deliberation. "I hadn't thought of it that way. But doesn't every female want a home and babies? And there's the money when you, ah, that is, from the Manor. What else could she want?"

"*En garde,* twig. You have a lot to learn."

Evan thought his father meant fencing, so he took up his position again. He was improving, too. In ten years or so he might be half as good as the older man.

Just when Evan thought he couldn't hold his arm up another minute, Holly entered the ballroom. As soon as Rendell lowered his sword, Evan thankfully let his blade rest on the ground. He'd never been so happy to see his old friend, even if she did look different. Her hair was tied in one long braid down her back, her spectacles were off, and she was wearing breeches. "Good grief, Hol, have you lost your mind?"

"No, Evan, I am trying to find it. I have just left the billiards room, where Papa"—she emphasized the last word, daring Evan to criticize the earl—"taught me how to play. Now I wish to learn to fence."

Two swords clattered to the floor.

Evan recovered first. He'd seen the breeches; Ren saw the woman in them. "Well, I ain't going to do it, Holly, for it ain't decent."

"I wasn't asking you."

Ren picked up both swords and wiped them with a towel before placing them in a case. He was *not* going to interfere between these two, he swore to himself again. Then he swore at himself, for letting his eyes slide down her delicately curving legs.

Evan was in a rant. "I'd expect something like this from your hey-go-mad sister, Holly, wanting to dress up in some stableboy's clothes and compete with men. I find the whole idea distasteful. Abhorrent. Almost sinful." And frightening, in case she turned out to be better at swordplay than he was. "Impossible."

Holly wasn't looking at him. "Papa agrees with me that a soldier's wife, if I should decide to be one, which I haven't, should know how to defend herself."

Evan knew better than to contradict the earl. The archbishop of Canterbury's word held less weight in this household. He snorted, though. "What are you defending yourself from, Holly, Berkshire heifers?"

"Who knows? I might end up following the drum. Officers' wives do not live in tents, nor do they wash their linens in rivers, contrary to what some people"—a glare at Evan—"would have me believe. What if our position was overrun by the enemy? How could I defend myself?"

"With your pistol, blast it! You're already a better shot than a female has a right to be."

"One pistol, one shot. Am I supposed to put it through my own heart, then?"

That was too much for even Ren's control. He'd seen war, and he'd seen its innocent victims. "I'll teach you."

All the ruffled feathers were smoothed by teatime the next day. Evan had apologized handsomely to Holly for losing his temper, and also to Merry, though it went against his grain. In return they'd let him win at spillikins last evening. Today, while the Carroll ladies were inspecting the village church to see what decorations would be needed for Christmas and the wedding, he'd gone shooting with the viscount. Killing a number of small, defenseless creatures had him in a better frame of mind, that and not knowing that Holly hadn't gone along with her mother and the others. If he thought at all about his father's comments on the advantages to Holly in their union, he merely counted fencing lessons in with not having to attend any more tedious debutante balls. If that was what she wanted, well, the old girl always had an odd kick to her gallop. It wasn't as if any Bond Street beaux were going to see her in men's garb, anyway, only his father.

After dinner, which included partridge pie, Evan was quick to point out, they all stood around the pianoforte singing. Holly played, but everyone joined in, the earl and countess included. Evan's contentment rose a notch, since his was far and away the best tenor voice. Why, his father could barely carry a tune and didn't know the words to half the songs. Evan grinned. Finally, finally, at last, Evan had found something he could do better than his father. The poor pater was reduced to sitting next to Holly on the bench, turning her pages. How boring. He mustn't be doing such a good job of that either, for Holly kept missing notes.

When they'd performed all the songs they knew, Lady Carroll declared it time to retire, with a busy day planned for the morrow: inventorying the linen closets before the wedding houseguests arrived. Her daughters groaned but dutifully said their good-nights. The countess herded her youngest girl upstairs with her, quickly followed by the earl, who gave a five-minute nod to Bartholemew. The butler was feeling mellow from the lovely singing, so decided to give the young couples ten. Joia and her viscount walked toward the stairs, just happening to find an opened door to an unoccupied parlor. They ducked inside as Bartholemew consulted his watch.

Rendell felt decidedly de trop. "I have some work to finish in the library. Good night, and thank you for a delightful evening, Lady Holly. Rest well, Evan, we'll practice with sabers tomorrow."

After his father left, Evan said, "It's early yet. I suppose I'll toddle off to the billiards room. Got to keep on top of my game if you're going to take up a cue stick, Hol." His smile showed he'd forgiven her for invading his domain.

"I'll walk with you." Holly removed her spectacles and fiddled with closing them as they went down the hall, past a frowning butler. "I think we should talk."

Evan selected a cue stick. He did not invite Holly to play, she noted. "If you think you can convince me to help your mother with the linen, you're dicked in the nob. I did that once, remember?"

"Yes, Mama made us both help after we put a frog in the governess's bed."

"I didn't put it there, and you know it."

"Yes, but you found the frog for me." Before he could claim that frightening the governess was her idea, which it was, and they got started on another brangle, she laid a hand on his arm. "That's not what I wanted to talk about."

"Deuce take it, Holly, you ruined my shot. And I don't see why you have to count linen, anyway, with a houseful of servants."

"The servants all have chores of their own, and Mama thinks— Oh, it doesn't matter. I wished to thank you for bringing Merry the collar for her dog. That was kind and thoughtful of you, Evan."

He made a shot from the other side of the table. "Devil take it, I never meant to make the chit cry. You never get weepy when we argue."

"No, but I'm used to your shouting," Holly said, following him around the table. "Merry's not. She didn't understand that you didn't mean anything by it."

"Fact is, I did, Hol. The chit's too forward by half. She hadn't ought to be working with the grooms in breeches, or riding with the hunt. And she shouldn't be playing billiards with the men." He held one hand up before she could interrupt. "I don't mean your father or Comfort. That's family. Like m'father showing you how to hold a sword. But that redheaded vixen is going to bring scandal on the house, you wait and see."

Holly supposed he thought Merry should be locked away in some man's pretty castle, too, raising sons and roses. Boredom would lead the minx into trouble that way for sure, but Evan was never going to understand. "Evan, kiss me."

The cue ball skipped off the table. After one lesson, Holly knew that wasn't good. "Dash it, Holly, don't say things like that. It's not proper."

"But I don't think it's proper to marry a man without knowing if you'll suit."

"Of course we suit, goose. We wouldn't be friends, else."

"I don't mean as companions, Evan. I mean as lovers."

Evan looked over his shoulder to make sure no servants were lingering in the vicinity. "You shouldn't be knowing anything about lovers."

"I know enough to understand that the heir your grandfather wants so badly isn't to be found under a cabbage leaf. And if . . . if two people do not care for each other in that way, they will both be unhappy in the marriage."

Evan's neckcloth appeared to be strangling him. His face was red and his hands were fumbling at his collar, billiards forgotten. "You're too bookish for your own good, Holly. You think too much, is what."

"I'm surprised you want to marry me, then."

"It's not a matter of wanting to, dash it. It's what all the parents and grandparents want. And there's Squire, saying I can't join up without starting a family." He noticed her picking up the discarded cue stick and backed out of range, though he could still feel the sparks from her eyes. "I mean, I like you, Holly. Always been my friend, don't you know."

"I have never made love with one of my friends."

"You haven't made love to anyone, goose. Uh, you haven't, have you?"

"Don't be more of a nodcock than you already are. If I knew how it was supposed to feel, I wouldn't be asking you."

His neckcloth was in tattered shreds, along with Evan's composure. "Thunderation, Holly, you can drive a fellow to Bedlam. First you don't know if you want to marry me, now you don't know if you want to make love with me."

"So kiss me."

So he did, a brief pressing of lips that left Holly unmoved. "That's it? That's what has Joia acting like a mooncalf? What poets write about? Bah!"

This was far worse than falling off a horse in front of one's prospective bride. This was falling off *and* getting kicked in the head. Evan tried again, harder. He pressed his lips harder to hers, he pressed her body closer to his. Holly felt nothing except her glasses breaking in her pocket. There was nothing offensive about Evan's kiss, no slobbering or pawing, no repulsive roughness. Nothing. She stepped back, having no inclination to continue the experiment, which, she decided, was conclusion enough.

"There," Evan was saying, proud to have left her speechless for once. "Told you we suited like cats and cream."

Holly squinted at him as he reracked the balls. Surely she hadn't missed something, had she? "Don't you think there should be more, ah, passion?"

"What, with one's wife? I should say not, Holly. A lady doesn't experience passion anyway. It's not the thing, don't you know. Didn't your mother tell you anything, old girl?"

When she wasn't disappearing around corners with Papa.

Chapter Seventeen

"*K*iss me, Ren." Holly had left Evan in the billiards room, saying she needed to think. Then, before she could lose her courage, she hurried past a disapproving Bartholemew into the library, without knocking, without stopping to consider her actions. "Please."

He'd risen at her entrance, but now sank back into his seat behind the desk. His coat was draped over the chairback, and his neckcloth hung loosely around his neck. Even so, like his son's before him, the blasted thing was suddenly too tight. Ren could barely swallow. "Excuse me?"

"I asked you to kiss me, sir." Holly was beside the desk, nervously rearranging the inkwell and the blotting paper. "And don't say you don't wish to, for I know otherwise. You're always so careful not to show your emotions, but I can tell by how you stared at my . . . person when we fenced, and tonight, when you were sitting next to me on the music bench, I know you felt the warmth when our thighs touched. And when you assisted me off my horse, you held me longer than necessary."

Rendell was sharpening his quill, down to the last row of barbs. "With all your experience with men, how do you know that means I want to kiss you?"

"Because I feel the same way."

His sharp intake of breath was all the answer she was going to get. Holly couldn't tell if her words had affected him or if he'd nicked his finger. "Do not patronize me, Ren. I am not a child."

As she leaned over the desk, the valley between her swelling breasts was at his eye level. "No, you are not a child, you are a beautiful young woman."

"And I deserve your honesty."

"I have never offered you anything but, *liebchen.* As I have never offered Evan anything less. Or did you forget about the whelp? I must admit I manage to ignore his existence for months on end, but not when his near-fiancée approaches me with such an outrageous request."

"I have just kissed Evan and we are not engaged."

"But you are as close to being betrothed as makes no difference. What kind of blackguard do you take me for, making advances to my son's chosen bride?"

"I am the one making advances, Ren, and I take you for an honorable man, which is why I asked in the first place."

"Do you even know what honor means, *liebchen,* to a man like me? A man who is not a gentleman?" He held up a hand when she would have protested. "I was not born a gentleman, one of the aristocracy. I was born on that thin line between gentry and tradesman. I had to be more honorable, more noble, than the bluest blue blood, just to join a schoolboys' club. That's why I was afraid to protest Blakely's entrapment, why I wed a chit I disliked and distrusted, because I wanted to be considered one of them, a gentleman. Now I am wealthy beyond their imaginings and therefore acceptable amongst the so-called Quality. But I find that I no longer care for their approval. I live by my own conscience, which has higher standards than the flirts and philanderers of the ton. No matter what I feel, no matter what you think you feel, you are my son's lady. So please leave me to my work. It's late."

"No, Ren, I am not leaving. I'm not flirting, and I'm not yet Evan's betrothed. I shall never be, either, unless you prove to me that passion is only a thing of poems, that intense emotions exist only in novels. Then I can settle for familiarity. What if I found out later, after I was wed, that I am of . . . of a warmer temperament than Evan? He assures me a lady does not entertain lustful thoughts."

"He is a jackass," Rendell muttered under his breath.

"I cannot go to a stranger with my doubts—that would truly land me in the basket—nor am I on such terms with Lord Comfort."

"I should hope not. As you guessed, passion should be reciprocal. I believe I heard Lady Joia threaten Comfort with a footstool if he so much as ogled a pretty serving girl."

"You see, you do understand. And you're experienced enough, I'm sure, for me to judge if there's more to kissing than lack of air, bumped noses, and bruised lips."

"The puppy really is a clunch if that's all he can manage." He smiled. "Perhaps Miss Blakely played me false after all."

"Then it will be perfectly acceptable for you to kiss me, as an experiment, a learning experience."

Like learning German and swordplay, the curious chit wanted to experiment with lovemaking. Ren eyed the open door, still seeking a reprieve. He was still a guest in her father's house. Abusing such trust was abhorrent to his ideals, yet his own curiosity was aroused, along with other parts of him. Lud, how he was tempted.

Holly went over and shut the door, turning the key in the lock before returning to his side. "I am not trying to trap you into anything, Ren. I am just trying to decide my entire future. I want to make a rational decision, evaluating all the factors, as it were."

"This is rational?"

"As it were. Reasonable, logical . . . lovely. Could we do that again, Ren? I'm not quite certain yet."

Bartholemew was quite certain that the library door ought to be unlocked. Five minutes and he'd go for the housekeeper's keys. Then again, Mr. Rendell was the most generous of guests, a gentleman to the tips of his expensively shod toes, despite his lack of a title. And Lady Holly was the sensible, trustworthy daughter, wasn't she?

* * *

Luncheon at Winterpark was an informal meal, with cold meats and cheeses placed on the sideboard for family and guests to help themselves. With the coming of winter, a tureen of soup or stew appeared, or a kidney pie. Today there were all three, since there were extra gentlemen in the house. Lord Carroll couldn't decide which he preferred, so he was having a helping of each. That was going to make Cook happier, since none of the younger men were present for the meal. Evan had taken himself hunting—no one had bothered to ask what—and Comfort was escorting Joia on social rounds, now that the linens were counted, with a maid and a footman in attendance. Mr. Rendell must be busy with his papers, the earl thought, knowing Bartholemew would see the man didn't go hungry.

"Well, this is nice for a change, just the family." He beamed at his wife and two youngest daughters. "We'll have to get used to being without our Joia soon anyway, won't we, Bess?"

Lady Carroll dabbed at her lips with her napkin. "We wouldn't be missing her so soon, if I had my way."

"Now, Bess," he began, but Holly started to say something, thank goodness. "You go ahead, poppet."

Holly took a deep breath. "Papa, Mama, I have decided to accept Rendell's proposal of marriage, with your permission."

"You've got it, my dear, of course. Couldn't be happier, in fact. Isn't that so, Bess?"

The countess was trying to put a good face on her disappointment. Merry didn't bother. "I think you could have done a lot— Ow."

"Your pardon, Lady Meredyth," Bartholemew said. "I must have stumbled against your chair. More tea?"

The earl was beaming. "So what finally made you see reason, poppet?"

"Reason had absolutely nothing to do with my decision, Papa, and I've come to see that it shouldn't. In fact, one kiss"—Holly didn't try to hide her blushes—"or perhaps more than one, and reason flies out the window. You never told me that, Papa."

127

"Meredyth, leave the room," the countess ordered, and was ignored.

"Eh? What's this? If that young jackanapes has been taking liberties before the vows are spoken, I'll—"

"No, Papa, not the young jackanapes. Didn't I say Rendell? Evan's father is the man I love and wish to marry."

Lord Carroll jumped to his feet, then sank back at the agony in his gouty big toe. "I'll see him dead first! That man is old enough to be your father, girl."

"Mr. Rendell is younger than you were when you married Mama. And I'm a year older than she was. Isn't that so, Mama?" Holly looked to her mother for support. She couldn't look to Merry, whose head was swiveling back and forth between Holly and their father, nor to Bartholemew, who was hiding his delight behind the serving dishes.

Lady Carroll answered, "Hollice is correct, Bradford. And she is a great deal wiser than I was at eighteen."

"Wiser? To throw her bonnet over the windmill for a regular here-and-thereian? The man is never in one place long enough to get his own mail!"

"Yes, isn't that glorious, Papa? I am finally going to see the places I've only read about, dreamt about. India, the Orient, the Indies. And Greece, Papa. Just think, I'll actually get to see the Acropolis. Perhaps Africa."

"He doesn't have a title." Lord Carroll conveniently forgot that Evan had been good enough for her without one.

"But he does have an outrageous amount of money and Prinny's ear if it matters so much to you. It doesn't to me, as long as I can be Mrs. Rendell."

The earl's face was turning an alarming purplish shade, so Lady Carroll hurriedly asked, "Do you love him then, my dear?"

If the stars in her eyes didn't tell the tale, her words did. "Oh, Mama, when I see him I can feel my heart beating faster. I want to be next to him, to touch him, to make him smile. He makes me want to write music, not just play it, so I can show him how much I do love him."

"And what about Evan?" her mother wanted to know, to make sure her daughter was certain. "What do you feel when you see him?"

"I feel like straightening his neckcloth or correcting his grammar. He's the best of good friends, and there is no better partner for charades. But I don't want to play games or act out what I am not."

"What about Evan's feelings?" the earl snapped. "You had an understanding."

Holly got up and went to her father's side, sitting on the arm of his chair as she used to do. "Papa, you and Squire Blakely had the understanding, not Evan and me. I love Evan like a brother, but I can talk to Ren, share my interests with him, and know he is going to respect my opinions. Isn't that a better foundation for marriage than lands marching together?"

"Evan was counting on you," Lord Carroll insisted, but his arm was around Holly's waist.

"Evan was counting on getting into the army. Ren is talking to Squire now, reminding him of Evan's youth and ambitions, his courage and patriotism. As a last resort, Ren says he'll offer the old grump ten thousand pounds to let Evan go. Evan will be in alt, for now he can apply for a position on Wellington's own staff. The general never wants married officers, it seems."

"That's all well and good for the young 'un, but why didn't Rendell come to me first?" The earl was determined to find something displeasing about the match.

"Because I went to him, Papa. And because he knows I can speak for myself."

Lady Carroll spoke up now: "I always thought Evan was too young for you, my dear, but we hardly know this man, his father. He seems like a fine gentleman, quiet and reserved, but why not take some time to get to know him before committing yourself? Perhaps in London for the spring? Then, at the end of the Season, if you decide you suit, you can have a proper year-long engagement and that beautiful wedding at Saint George's the following May or June. Then you'll be sure."

"I'm sure now, Mama, and I don't wish to have even one

dance with another man. Ren is off to Vienna after Christmas, and he already has a special license."

The countess threw her serviette on the table. "I won't hear of it."

"But Joia won't mind a double wedding. We spoke of it all the time, as girls."

"I mind, Hollice. I mind very much that another of my daughters would get married in a harum-scarum ceremony."

Ren came into the room then, still rubbing his hands, which were chilled from the cold ride to Squire's and the faster ride back. He bowed to the countess. "I am sorry, my lady, to displease you. I know you do not wish to part with your daughter, but what can I say to convince you? Would it matter if I swear that I love her with all my heart, that I shall cherish her forever? I had no choice the first time, and no marriage to speak of. It has taken me all these many years to find a woman to trust, a woman to share my life with, my travels, my thoughts, my children. Evan was cheated of a father the first time, and I of a son. All I can do for him now is ease his way in the army, let him make his own choices. But I want to have a family, a real family, and I cannot wait much longer if I'm to show Holly the world, make a home for her out of Rendell Hall, and then help her fill it with our children. She deserves to have what she wants out of life, too, doesn't she?"

Coming to stand next to Ren, Holly put her hand in his. "I want him, Mama, no other."

Lady Carroll was crying happy tears into her napkin, and Merry was cheering. Lord Carroll conceded. "Can't say that I like the arsy-varsy way this match came about, but if it makes you happy, poppet, you have my blessing. Let's have a toast."

Bartholemew was already pouring.

Lord and Lady Carroll were snuggled in the sofa in their private sitting room late that night. Bess had finished weeping for the lost dream wedding, and she hadn't yet begun cataloging the havoc this new arrangement would wreak on her existing plans. That would come tomorrow.

"Promise me, Bradford, that you won't push Meredyth into any hasty match. She's much too young."

"Of course not, my dear. The gal ain't ready for marriage. She needs a bit more time."

"She's only seventeen. She needs at least two or three Seasons before she'll know enough of the world to make a wise choice."

Two or three Seasons? Lord Carroll had other plans. "Did you ever stop to think, my dear, that our Merry mightn't take in London? I mean, I think she's top drawer, but London?"

"Nonsense, of course she'll be a success. She is a well-bred, well-educated, well-behaved child."

"And she's well and away the most headstrong and impulsive deb ever to make her bows. Think of all the pitfalls for a lass like Merry in Town, all the silly rules she won't deem worthy of obeying. No gallops in Hyde Park, no talking to unintroduced strangers. Why, the chit is as friendly as her pup! And that's another thing: if she brings that dog along, you'll have merry mayhem, indeed."

Lady Carroll's cheeks paled and her hand trembled as she tucked it more firmly into her husband's. "She'll mature," she said, loyal to the end.

"Didn't take Holly that long to know her own mind, did it? Maybe we'll get lucky with missy, too."

"I do believe we are fortunate in Mr. Rendell, Bradford. He's such a quiet, intelligent gentleman that I feel he's quite one of the family already. He adores Hollice, and he doesn't have any troublesome, toplofty relatives like Comfort does."

"And he's rich as Croesus. Not that Holly chose him for the blunt, but a money tree in the family isn't a bad thing, not at all."

"I'm just glad Hollice didn't settle on Evan, the way you were urging her."

"Me? Urging her to take that moonling? It was you, pushing them together at every turn. The boy's too young, too much a glory-seeker. No, I never meant him for my girl. Why do you think I invited the nabob?"

PART THREE

The Silent Knight

Chapter Eighteen

"*B*-but I ain't in the p-p-petticoat line, Evan. You know I d-d-d—"

"Don't talk well with them," Evan finished for his friend. "Deuce take it, Max, you're one of the heroes of the Peninsula, and Prinny just knighted you for bravery. How can you get in such a quake over a Christmas house party?"

Sir Max, until recently Lieutenant Maxwell Grey of His Majesty's Cavalry, could have told his friend that it wasn't the party that had him in such a panic, not the good food and wassail, not the gathering of Yuletide greenery. It was the daughters of the house—and there always were daughters, or nieces, or neighbors' girls—who had his nerves in more knots than it took to truss the Christmas goose. Max could have explained his dilemma to Evan, that is, if he weren't so tongue-tied at the very thought of accompanying his friend to Berkshire and then to the festivities at Winterpark, home to three young persons of the female persuasion. He did manage to say, "You know th-the knighthood w-was an accident."

"So what? No one else has to know, and besides, it's the title before your name that counts. At least you earned yours, you didn't just inherit it. And you can't deny you deserve all the ribbons on your chest."

Evan stopped his packing to admire the decorations on his friend's dress uniform. He'd have his own medals soon, Evan thought, as soon as this blasted wedding nonsense was over.

Meantime, he looked fine in his fresh-from-the-tailors scarlet regimentals, if he had to say so himself. Max's uniform, for all its trophies, showed signs of wear, a spot here, a frayed edge there. Of course, there was no sense in Max ordering a new outfit, not when he was just waiting for his resignation papers to be processed. If Max hadn't been ordered out of the army by the physicians after his last injury, they'd be going off to fight the war together. Instead, they were going to Berkshire.

"You don't have to talk, old man. Most of the time we'll be at m'grandfather's place anyway. Winterpark's too crowded with the wedding guests. When we do go there, just stand around and look heroic. You'll do." And he would, too, Evan thought with a pang of envy at his friend's erect carriage and classical good looks. At one and twenty, Max was two years Evan's senior, and besides having had four years ahead of Evan to prove himself in the army, he was taller and broader of shoulder. He was too thin from his recent wound, and his hair was an unfortunate shade of red, but Max did look fine in all that gold braid. "Women swoon over a chap in uniform."

Good grief, Max worried, would he be expected to catch them? "I'm n-not going. T-too much t-to d-d—"

"You've got nothing better to do, Max. You told me yourself. You can't spend Christmas here in the barracks all alone. That's too dismal a thought."

After the last injury, Max knew he'd been granted a reprieve by the Grim Reaper. Nothing was too dismal for a man who'd felt Death's breath on his cheek. He hadn't lost his leg to the French cannon, and he hadn't lost his life to the infection that followed. He was left with a weakness to the lungs that might go away or might not, according to the military sawbones, making him useless to the army. It didn't help his speech impediment either. So what? He would be content to be alive and out of the hospitals—if he didn't have to go to a wedding party in Berkshire.

"Besides," Evan was going on, without interrupting his packing, "the air here in Town can't be any good for you. All that soot and fog. I hear you coughing, nights. Decent fresh country air, that's what you need. And exercise for your leg.

136

I'm always given free welcome at Lord Carroll's stables, the finest in the county, don't you know. Winterpark's got capital hunt country, or, if the ground's too hard, there's an indoor jumping ring to keep his horses fit. You'll love it."

"B-b—"

"And if you're planning on taking over that bit of land you inherited, you could do worse than consult with Lord Carroll. The earl knows more about husbandry than anyone you're liable to meet. And he's not a bit high in the instep."

Max stared at the open, empty suitcase on his own bed. "B-but he's got d-d—"

"Daughters, I know. Three of them. You don't have to worry, old chap, they're all good sports, and Carroll ain't looking to get you legshackled to any of them. He held out for a duke's heir for Joia, and m'father for Holly. The pater's a nabob, don't you know. They'll be happy as grigs jaunting around." He shrugged. "No accounting for tastes. So that only leaves Merry, and she's too young. No offense, old man, but you've got your knighthood and your medals, that scrap of unproductive land, and two cousins ahead of you before you can hope for a peerage or an inheritance. That's not much to recommend you to a prospective papa as particular as the earl."

The earl's daughters could look to the highest in the land, Max thought, and had. They'd never notice a broken-down soldier. He could ride and relax, eat better food than he'd had in four years, maybe ask the earl to recommend some books about agriculture. Max took a pile of neatly folded shirts out of his drawer.

But what if the daughters had friends? They were bound to be popular. Evan said they were great guns, decent enough sorts that he'd been prepared to marry one of them. It was a wedding; there'd be bridesmaids. Max would have to do the pretty with a houseful of females. Scores of them. Maybe hundreds. Max pictured himself trying to navigate his way through a shop filled with china shepherdesses, blindfolded, with his hands tied behind his back. Mounted on a horse. He put the shirts back in his drawer.

Evan took them out again and tossed them haphazardly

toward Max's suitcase. "Deuce take it, I need you with me, old man. It'll be deadly dull in the country, else, with no one at Blakely Manor but m'grandparents. Truth to tell, m'grand-father ain't best pleased with me right now. He'll come around, of course, when he sees I don't perish at the first engagement, but I intend to play least in sight at the Manor. At Winterpark there'll be the two pairs of lovebirds and the infant. No one to ride out with or go to the tavern with when they start talking wedding plans. I have to stand witness for my father—glad to do it, don't you know, pleased as punch he asked—but I don't want anyone thinking I'm wearing the willow for Holly or any-thing. You've got to come, Max."

So Sir Maxwell, recently, and if he had his druthers, still, Lieutenant Grey, traveled with his barracks-mate into Berkshire, or into hell, depending on who was reading the signposts.

Max survived his introduction to the Blakelys easily enough. The old squire stormed out of the room and Mrs. Blakely wept on Evan's new jacket. Then they went to Winterpark for dinner.

The modest house where Max was raised could have fit into the entry hall of Lord Carroll's family seat. Max's self-confidence could have fit into a peapod, one with a wormhole in it, so the contents dribbled away when the most dignified personage in the world greeted them. And that was only the butler.

Evan duly presented Max to three vibrant, exquisite young women—four if one included their mother, who was every-thing gracious, trying to set him at ease. She might have defeated Boney single-handedly more easily. He did manage to lift the ladies' hands the proper two inches beneath his lips when they held them out to him. He made creditable bows when they didn't, as was the case with the Duchess of Carlisle.

"Don't mind the old besom," Evan whispered to Max. "She's such a dragon, her own husband don't live at home. Comfort's mother, don't you know."

In addition to the other guests, Max also had to meet the viscount, a Corinthian of the first stare; his father, the duke; Evan's father, the nabob; and the young ladies' father, the earl. What the deuce was Max Grey doing in this elevated assemblage? Trembling, that's what.

Since they were gathered in the Chinese Room before dinner, Max decided to take up a position in front of one of the red lacquer screens in the corner, hoping his regimentals would blend in. His camouflage must have worked, for no one addressed Max except a footman serving sherry, which the officer declined. Dutch courage was not his way. Dying the slow death of a social misfit was, in spades. There was no way in Hades he was going to last through this night, much less two weeks. He'd only embarrass himself and Evan, so it was better if he made his excuses now. He'd march right up to Lady Carroll, in front of all of these polished and pomaded paragons, and announce he had to leave before he puked. Pigs would fly first.

So Max stood at attention. He was on guard duty, ready to defend his Chinese screen, or crawl behind it. Then the enemy approached. "Lieutenant Grey? Or should it be Sir Maxwell? I'm to be your dinner partner." Merry tucked her arm into his and led Max into the dining room.

The room could have seated half his battalion, but Max was no more intimidated than he'd been earlier, since he'd passed the point of panic. He was going to have to speak to this young woman. And the woman on his other side. Lud, he should have thrown himself on that French cannon.

Miss Merry chattered away, though, getting them through the first course. No, Max had to remind himself, Evan's familiarity wasn't his. She was Lady Meredyth, as hard as it might be to think of such a lively little sprite possessing such a starched-up title. She looked more like a forest elf with her wide green eyes and cap of red curls. Her hair wasn't as carroty as his, Max noted, but was a richer, darker shade of auburn. Her mouth seemed curved in a permanent smile, when she wasn't talking about her father's hunters, her dog, or Evan's military career.

Then it was time for Max to turn to his other dinner partner, a woman of a certain age named Miss Almira Krupp, who was companion to the Duchess of Carlisle, poor thing. Miss Krupp was far more interested in Reverend Foster on her other side—the widowed Reverend Foster on the other side of fifty—than an impecunious cavalry castoff.

Miss Krupp's defection suited Max down to his toes, which were beginning to uncurl in his boots. Now he could enjoy his meal in peace. After years of stringy chicken roasted on a stick over an open fire—when the soldiers could find a chicken or light a fire—this meal was heavenly. Lady Meredyth kept urging him to try this or that delicacy, and then didn't mind when his mouth was too full for conversation. The girl seemed satisfied, in fact, with a nod or a smile or a "Hmm" to whatever she was speaking about at the moment. Right now she was talking about the coming wedding.

"I'm to be the only bridesmaid, you see, now that Holly is one of the brides, and Mama is furious. She says it's uncivilized and a poor reflection on the family. What do you think, Sir Max?"

He grunted.

"No, I don't think so either. But then there's the problem of Holly's gown. It was to be red velvet, for the Christmas wedding, but Mama says no self-respecting bride gets married in a red gown, and there's no time to have another fitted. Mama is having a white lace overdress made to cover the red velvet. Isn't that clever?"

He nodded.

"Yes, I thought so, too. Even if Papa complains the stuff costs enough to be made of spun gold. Um, I'm not boring you, am I? Papa says my tongue runs on wheels."

Max shook his head vehemently. He wanted to ask what she was going to wear, but was afraid to press his luck. She ought to be dressed in green, he thought, to match her sparkling eyes. Then she'd look more like a woodland pixie than ever.

"My gown is green velvet," she said, as if reading his mind. Max said, "Ah."

* * *

After dinner the young people played charades, heaven and Evan be praised. Strutting like the cock of the rock in his uniform, Evan picked Max and Merry to be on his team, leaving Holly with Joia and the viscount, who had eyes for no one but each other. Mr. Rendell had to complete some business, he said, and the older members of the party were setting up two tables for whist, the duke at one table, the duchess at the other.

Max didn't do half badly at charades. Of course, by the time he managed to utter his guess to the clues, Lady Meredyth or Evan had shouted out the answer. When it was his turn to act out a phrase or a bit of poetry, Max performed nobly. Silently and blushingly, but nobly. They lost anyway.

The poker-backed butler wheeled in the tea cart piled high with sweets and nuts and fruit. The duke sat at one end of the room and the duchess held court at the other, and neither was interested in Max, thank goodness. He planned to keep eating so he wouldn't be called upon to make conversation. He might get through this evening yet.

Later Evan went off with Comfort to play billiards, and Max would have gone along, too, but Lady Meredyth took his arm and led him to her father.

"Papa, here is Sir Maxwell. Evan says he is going to need advice about some land he's going to try to make productive."

Lord Carroll's gout was bothering him. So was the duke, who wouldn't reconcile with his wife, not even for the duration of the wedding party. Poor Bess had the headache from trying to keep Their Graces apart and entertained. The earl could tell she was suffering from across the room. Which meant he'd be sleeping in his own bed tonight, damn them all. Evan's friend could grow kippered herring for all the earl cared right now. "Go find him Coke's pamphlets, missy. That's the best place to start. And then, young sir, you might as well listen to Merry's opinions. The gal knows more about estate management and good husbandry than half the bailiffs I've employed."

Max bowed and left, smiling. He might just survive the whole two-week house party.

Chapter Nineteen

*L*ady Carroll was not about to let her daughters go off without the proper monograms on their linens. So what if both of their husbands-to-be could purchase entire haberdasheries? A lady was known by her fancy needlework, and hurried weddings or not, Joia and Hollice would have their embroidered handkerchiefs and pillowslips. Besides, sewing in the countess's sitting room, they could all hide from the difficult duchess and her crosspatch companion. Bess gave another silent prayer of gratitude that Aunt Irmentrude wasn't coming for the weddings. That old crone would think nothing of invading the countess's private chambers.

Those rooms overlooked the sweeping lawns and carriage drive of Winterpark, so Merry, in the window seat, could watch the gentlemen set off for a ride. "Isn't he divine?" she asked no one in particular because she knew the answer.

"Who, Merry?" Joia asked, looking up from her stitching, sure her youngest sister meant Viscount Comfort.

Knowing that her own handsome fiancé had driven over to Rendell Hall to start the renovations, Holly said, "I hope you don't mean Evan, Merry. I know he looks dashing in his uniform, but it wouldn't do for you to form a *tendre* for him. He may be one of my oldest friends and my stepson in two weeks, which I have a hard time comprehending myself, but I do have to admit that he's as unsteady as ever."

"Not Evan, silly." Merry looked back into the room, now

that the gentlemen had ridden out of sight. "The lieutenant. Sir Maxwell. You should see how well he sits a horse. He's a much better rider than Evan."

"You're a better rider than Evan, mitten," Joia teased, using their old pet name for the baby of the family. "But surely you cannot be serious about the officer."

"Why not? He's everything marvelous." She began a catalog of Sir Max's endowments with his attractive looks.

Joia laughed. "Only you would think so, mitten, with that gingery mop."

Merry tossed her head, red curls flying. "And he's got lovely broad shoulders and elegant legs."

"Not as broad as Craighton's."

"Not as well muscled as Ren's."

"Girls!" their mother scolded. "We are not judging a horse fair."

The others answered, "Yes, Mama," and went back to their sewing, but Merry didn't, which was no great loss to the trousseaux as her stitches were uneven and her threads were always breaking. She was determined to defend the lieutenant. "Evan says he suffered grievous injuries and fevers. That's why he's not up to his usual weight, so his clothes hang loosely. We have to fatten him up again."

"What, is he to be the Christmas goose?" Holly teased.

"He could be," Joia added, "for all his social graces. I'm sorry, mitten, but I've had better conversations with the clothespress."

Merry was scowling. "How can you both make fun of one of our nation's bravest soldiers? Did you see all of his medals and commendations? He was wounded in *our* defense. Why, our own Prince Regent knighted him for valor."

"Don't be a widgeon," Holly said with a laugh. "Evan told me the right of that story. Your valiant warrior didn't perform any great feat of derring-do; he saved Prinny's favorite hound from being run over by a carriage. The prince was above par, as per usual, and wanted to promote your lieutenant on the spot, but Grey had already submitted his resignation papers. Prinny had to knight him because he'd promised a reward in front of the entire parade ground, and of course, His Majesty doesn't have a groat to his name."

"Well, I still think he was brave. A man who will risk his life for a dog is to be admired. Your gentlemen"—she glared at her sisters—"can barely risk the tassels on their Hessians with Downsy."

"Goodness, I believe mitten is smitten," Joia said, and Holly joined in her laughter. Their mother, however, was not smiling. Her youngest daughter could not be old enough for calf love.

"Sir Maxwell is of good family," she said, when Meredyth appeared ready to toss her sewing at the two grinning girls. "Although he is from the cadet branch."

"And he is well enough looking, I suppose," Holly admitted, also to placate her sister. "If you don't mind red hair."

"He must have performed bravely in the Peninsula to have won all those ribbons," Joia contributed. She couldn't be less than truthful, however, so she had to add, "But I'm sorry, mitten. The man is a block."

Before Merry could jump to her knight's defense, Holly quickly put in, "Evan swears the man isn't stupid. He's simply backward in company."

As a child, Merry was the happiest creature around. When she wasn't happy, however, everyone knew it. Lady Carroll could feel the headache coming on just thinking about one of her baby's rages. To this day, Aunt Irmentrude was a picnic in the park compared to Meredyth in a miff. "Enough, girls. We'll never get the sewing finished at this rate. Meredyth, you are far behind. Joia, Hollice, do please remember that it is impolite to belittle another's handicap. Sir Maxwell is neither bacon-brained nor badly behaved. He stutters, is all."

Merry looked from one to the other. "He does?"

Max couldn't keep up with Evan on the morning's ride. He could, that is, if he didn't mind setting his recovery back a week. So he returned to Winterpark with the borrowed horse, a prime goer and a real pleasure, he told the men in the stables, with no hesitation. He could have ridden on to Blakely Manor on his own mount, but didn't fancy the chill reception he'd get there. Instead he asked one of the grooms to direct him to Lord Carroll's library via a rear door, thinking he could hide out there until Evan returned.

The door was open, so he walked in, to the surprise of Evan's father and his betrothed, who were doing something on top of the architectural plans on the desk, and it wasn't making notations.

Oh Lud. Max couldn't simply back out, for they'd seen him, and Mr. Rendell was looking thunderclouds. Max couldn't blame the man, but dash it, they could have closed the door. He did stare at the shelves of books nearest him while Lady Holly straightened her spectacles and her bodice. She didn't bother with her hair. "Were you looking for someone?" she asked in a kindly tone, taking pity on him for her sister's sake.

"C-Coke."

"Oh yes, the agronomist. I think Papa keeps those volumes over here. Evan said you inherited a bit of property you wanted to farm. Where is it?"

"K-Kent."

"And you were hoping to grow . . . ?"

"C-cows." Because her laughing eyes seemed friendly enough, Max took a deep breath and added, "And mangel-wurzels." They both sighed in relief when he got that out. By now, however, beads of perspiration were forming on Max's forehead. All he wanted to do was get the book and leave these two to their privacy before Evan's father skewered him for the interruption.

Misunderstanding his distress and concerned over his pallor, Holly took a book down from the shelf and urged him into a chair. "You sit here, sir. I'll go fetch help."

Help would have been two miles between Max and the mogul. Instead Holly fetched Lady Merry, who sent for a footman, who brought a tray of scones and biscuits. "Here, I'll read while you eat, Sir Max," the auburn-haired angel said. "Just nod if you have a question."

The question was whether his horse was going to be able to carry him back to Blakely's.

* * *

Informal dancing was to be that evening's entertainment at Winterpark. Additional young people, friends of the various Carroll daughters, had been invited from nearby to make up the sets. The friends' parents joined the elders at cards, helping to amuse Their Graces. The duchess was pleased as punch to lord it over the local gentry, while the duke set up a flirt with a plump widow. Lady Carroll having refused his advances, the duke had been at loose ends. He'd almost been at the end of Lord Carroll's steel, long friendship, gouty foot, children's marriage, and all. Now Carlisle was happier about being stuck in the country, especially since his wife was watching, and the widow was ten years younger than Her Grace. He made sure he led the cozy armful out for a waltz between card games, too.

Max wasn't dancing. He could dance, but he couldn't dance and make conversation at the same time, as expected by the giddy debs he'd partnered in the past. He'd borrowed a page from Lord Carroll's book, therefore, and brought his cane along, the cane he hadn't used or needed for over a fortnight. Then he wrote a chapter of his own by tapping his chest and coughing whenever someone approached him and asked why he wasn't dancing. Lady Joia thought to introduce him to some of the local lasses, who were clearly delighted that the comeliest competition in the neighborhood was finally being taken out of the lists. Max coughed.

Evan swirled by, a pretty girl in his arm. She was wearing a pink gown with too many bows, Max decided, like a gift package tied by a War Office committee. The Carroll ladies all wore simple gowns that fell straight from high waistlines, adorned with bits of lace and ribbon. When Evan led the confection his way at the end of the set, Max coughed.

He would have sat by Lady Holly at the pianoforte, turning her pages, but Mr. Rendell was there, demanding a dance, so Miss Almira Krupp, the duchess's companion, took her place. Max backed away, coughing. The butler kept sending footmen his way with glasses of lemonade. Max hated lemonade, but he felt better with something in his hand, not so conspicuously shirking his social duties, so he drank it anyway. Then he could waste some more time visiting the necessary.

When he returned, however, Miss Krupp was playing a waltz. The duke was dancing with his new light-o'-love. Viscount Comfort and Mr. Rendell partnered their betrotheds. Evan twirled around another fussily dressed female who was obviously enamored of his uniform. And Merry, Lady Meredyth, was being held in a too tight embrace by a gangly youth in high shirt points and padded shoulders. She was talking nineteen to the dozen and the juvenile—Max could see his spotty complexion—was laughing back as they swooped and swirled the length of the drawing room. Max choked, for real.

"May I fetch you something, Sir Maxwell?" the butler asked, appearing at Max's side on the instant. "Hot tea? Perhaps one of Cook's tisanes?"

Next the old fellow would be asking if he needed a mustard plaster for his chest, by Jupiter, Max fretted, and loudly enough for the company to hear over Miss Krupp's playing. But the downy old butler's eyes were twinkling, Max noted, so he nodded. Yes, there was something Mr. Bartholemew could do for him. Max tipped his head in the companion's direction. "Another w-waltz?" he asked, half pleading.

Bartholemew whispered to Lady Joia, who, with a glance in Max's direction, relieved Miss Krupp at the pianoforte. "I've been wanting to play this new score I just purchased," he heard her tell the scrawny spinster. "I hope no one minds that it's another waltz."

Having seen some of the byplay, Mr. Rendell minded that he couldn't hold his beloved for one more dance, to please some plaguey stray pup Evan had dragged home. Then Holly patted the bench beside her and smiled up at him. Ren relaxed. This was better than a dance. The whelp was forgiven and forgotten.

Max didn't notice. He was making his way across the room to where Merry stood among a circle of befrilled females and their feckless swains. "M-my dance?" he asked, holding his hand out to her in front of them all, proving he really was a brave soul.

If she glowed like candlelight before, Max thought, Merry's

answering grin was a whole bonfire, warming him to the bones.

"I thought you weren't dancing because of your chest, old man." Evan was trying to be helpful. Max kicked him, behind his partner's skirts.

"I'm sure one dance won't hurt, will it?" Merry asked hopefully.

No, it wouldn't hurt. Holding Merry in his arms, feeling her touch on his shoulder, Max couldn't breathe, he couldn't feel his game leg, and his heart seemed to be beating louder than the music. It felt glorious.

Chapter Twenty

"*I* am worried about that man, Bradford."

Lord Carroll patted his wife's knee, there on the sofa beside him late that night. "What are you worried about, Bess, that the duke will cause a scandal in the neighborhood with Thaddeus Brady's widow? Don't fatch yourself, my love. Carlisle is only acting the rake to rile that sour prune he's married to. He knows what's due his name and distinction, and his son's bride. Just today Carlisle told me that he thinks our Joia is the perfect wife for the viscount. No niminy-piminy miss, he called her," the earl related proudly. " 'Od's truth, she'll keep Comfort from following in his father's wandering footsteps, if that's the man you're fussing about."

"No, not Comfort and not his father. The man I referred to is the friend of Evan's who has our Meredyth moonstruck, that young officer."

Lord Carroll sipped at his wine. He was allowed one glass these days, so he would be in condition to walk his daughters down the aisle without his cane. He meant to make that glass last, and this, too, his favorite time of day with Bess—unless he counted the moments after, when he followed her to her bedroom, or she to his. Or when he woke in the morning with her head on his shoulder, all warm and rosy. These days she was out of his bed at dawn, it seemed, she was so busy with the wedding plans, the house party, and preparations for Christmas. Bess might be marrying not one but two daughters off to

149

nonpareils, but the tenants would have their baskets, the servants would have their Boxing Day gifts, the children of their dependents would have their treats. Lord Carroll patted Bess's leg again. What a good wife she was, what a good friend. He'd give her the stars and moon if he had them. He did have the son. . . .

"Bradford, this is no time for wool-gathering. What are you going to do about that man, Sir Maxwell Grey?"

"What would you have me do, my love, tell Comfort to toss him out into the cold? Ask Rendell to challenge the boy to a duel? Good thing to have around, sons-in-law, when a suitor goes beyond the line. Thing is, young Grey hasn't overstepped himself, has he, Bess?"

"Of course not, Bradford. I'm not implying Sir Maxwell is not a gentleman."

"I'm glad, for I'd hate to see the last of him. He seems a decent lad to me. Good head on his shoulders, good seat on a horse, and good, solid plans for his future. He's a steadying influence on that firebrand Evan."

"I am not concerned with the man's influence on Evan. It's his effect on Meredyth that has me worried. You said yourself she's too young to think of marrying."

"Calf love, my dear. No one is talking about marrying them off."

"Talking's another thing. The man is so . . . shy."

"Is he?" Lord Carroll took another sip. "He didn't seem so to me. We had a long coze about sheep and hogs after you ladies left the dining room."

The countess tried not to frown—she didn't want more wrinkles before the wedding—but she knew what her husband was like when on one of his hobbyhorses. "Did you let the man get a word in edgewise?"

"Of course. It was Grey asking the questions, after all. He seems to be a quick learner, asked intelligent questions. No, I wouldn't say he was shy. Mayhaps he's only that way around the ladies. Been raised by uncles, don't you know, then school and the army. Can't hold it against a cove if he's not a ladies' man."

"No, but—"

"And he's bold enough when he needs to be. Did you see the way he waded through mitten's circle of beaux to claim her for that waltz?"

That was what had Lady Carroll in a flutter. It was one thing for her baby to indulge in hero worship, quite another when the unlikely hero returned the compliment. "Everyone saw it. Even the duchess commented."

"Well, a good soldier knows when to go on the offense. He had a fine leg, too, for a wounded soldier. I thought you said he limped."

"He did," Bess answered wryly, "before that waltz."

The earl chuckled. "So that's the way of it, eh? Our little tomboy has an admirer. She had to make the jump into a woman sometime, Bess."

"Yes, but I'm afraid she'll throw her heart over the first fence. You know how she's always bringing home unfortunate creatures? I fear she thinks of Sir Maxwell as another of her strays."

The earl patted his wife's hand once more and kissed the worry lines on her forehead. "If it will make you feel any better, I'll take the boy around the estate with me this week. I'll tell him he'll learn more from the tenant farmers than from books, which is God's own truth. Between that and riding out with Evan, the lad'll be too tuckered out to get up to trouble when he is around. Besides, my love, it's only for another two weeks."

"A lot can happen in two weeks."

Max was gratified when a messenger from the earl arrived at Blakely Manor during breakfast the next morning. He'd feared to appear too inquisitive, too encroaching, but now the earl was inviting him to ride along on his rounds of Winterpark's fields and farms. Max was fascinated by what he saw: the modern equipment, the variety of livestock, the respect the tenants had for their lord. Sometimes in Spain he'd wondered just what he was fighting to preserve. This was it.

Lord Carroll was also impressed. Here was no dilettante, no Town dandy, no well-bred whopstraw too full of himself to get his hands dirty and too arrogant to appreciate a humble farmer's wisdom. Perhaps the war had given the lieutenant a maturity well beyond his years, or perhaps his brush with death had taught him the value of life. Lord Carroll could understand, thinking of his own mortality.

The earl was also thinking that, if Bess was right about Merry—and she was usually right about everything—this Sir Max might be a godsend. He'd have to ask Bartholemew's opinion when they got back.

That afternoon the gentlemen were sent out to collect Christmas greenery for the ladies to weave into garlands and wreaths and kissing boughs. The butler had wrapped an additional muffler around Max's neck, and the earl checked twice to make sure he wasn't tiring himself out, dragging yew branches to the wagons. How kind everyone was, Max thought, and how foolish he'd been to dread coming to the house party.

He enjoyed himself that evening also, when he and Evan stopped at Winterpark after dinner in time to join in singing Christmas carols. Amazingly enough, Max could sing. Somehow, when he knew the words and the music, the sounds simply flowed from his tongue. It had always been thus, so he wasn't the least nervous about lifting his rich baritone in counterpoint to Evan's tenor and the lovely sopranos of the Carroll sisters. One silvery voice in particular made music hum through his veins.

Max slept well that night from all the exercise, and from one bright-eyed pixie singing in his sweet, sweet dreams.

The following day brought sleet, a miserable cold dampness that wavered between rain and snow. Max's leg was bothering him—the sawbones had warned it would in bad weather—and he was happy to sit by the Squire's fire with the books he'd borrowed from Winterpark's library. Evan, though, was bored and irritable. Gone were the days when he could drop in on his friend Holly and her sisters for a game or a chat. Gone, too, were the fencing lessons. Evan's father was spending most of his time at Rendell Hall with Holly, planning the renovations for when they returned from their travels. Evan wasn't bookish, Max's leg was too stiff for swordwork, and Blakely Manor didn't have a billiards room.

"Hell and damnation," Evan swore when he lost another round of patience. "If it weren't for this blasted wedding, I could already be on my way to the front."

Where one was also damp and cold, or hot and dry, for days on end with nothing to do, Max warned. He was hoping Evan could find something to occupy his time and mind; he wanted to finish this book.

They were both glad when a note came from Lord Carroll asking if they could come help exercise the horses in the indoor ring. With so many guests and so many carriages, Winterpark's grooms were overwhelmed. The earl didn't want any of his high-bred beauties going sour in their stalls.

Joia was preparing to lead a group of Comfort's relatives on a tour of the house.

"I don't know how you stand it," Merry told her sister. "There are Ellingsworths coming out of the woodwork, to say nothing of the duchess's relations, who have to be kept apart now, too."

"Comfort promises we only have to see them twice a year, and not both sides of the family at once. His mother never comes to London and his father never goes to Bath. I do think that is why he's so keen on a place of his own in Ireland, though, and a long honeymoon trip."

Merry knew Comfort had more interesting things in mind for that honeymoon than avoiding his family. She sighed, wondering if any man would ever look at her like the last oasis in a barren desert.

At the sound of despondency, Lord Carroll looked up from his newspaper. "Why so long-faced, mitten? Nothing to do?

I'm promised to the duke for a chess game, but why don't you visit the stables, see how Jake and the lads are doing with all the extra cattle? I'm sure Jake would be pleased if you took a few turns around the exercise ring with some of the young 'uns. We don't want them getting away—that is, getting lazy."

The Spanish Riding Academy couldn't rival this place, Max thought. Dozens of horses could be schooled on lunge lines at one end, and another score or so taken over jumps at the other end. The vast arena had mirrors along the walls so a rider could check his own performance as well as the horses'. No wonder Evan claimed that all of the Carrolls were such superb equestrians. How could they not be, with such magnificent horseflesh and such a training field?

Having appraised Max's skill yesterday, the head groom, Jake, gave him one of the few young stallions kept for riding. " 'E's a rare 'andful, 'e is, but worth the effort."

Atlas was one of the sweetest goers Max had ever ridden, once he'd shaken the fidgets out. The big chestnut was fast and agile, responsive and eager. He'd make a steeplechase winner for sure, Max thought, if he didn't get the bit between his teeth. Keeping Atlas to a controlled cadence took all of Max's concentration, beyond noting the other riders, grooms and smallish jockeys, a grinning Evan on a rangy gray.

Max and Atlas were sailing over the jumps as if they were knee-high instead of shoulder height, so Jake came and raised some of the bars. Now even the big horse had to pay attention.

They were flying. Evan and some of the grooms had pulled up to watch them take one last circuit of the hurdles. Max showed Atlas the next obstacle and started to collect him for the jump when, from the corner of his eye, he saw another rider racing toward the same barrier. The fellow could deuce well turn aside, Max decided. He wasn't giving up the jump and there wasn't room for two horses across.

But then—Lud, why did he have to look?—Max spotted auburn curls under the other rider's knit cap. Breeches and boots, though—no, it couldn't be. She wouldn't. She would. And a gentleman always yielded to a lady.

Max pulled Atlas's head over at the last second, turning the horse to make way for Merry and her roan gelding. Atlas made the instantaneous maneuver with no problem except the insult to his dignity, which he showed by going up on his hind legs.

Max was in the wrong position, looking over his shoulder to make sure Merry's horse made the jump. The next thing he knew, he was sailing over the bars after her, without his horse.

Merry and Evan were running toward him almost before Max hit the ground. First he heard the sound of his leg snapping under him, then he heard the two of them screaming at each other.

"Look what you've done now, you blasted hoyden. You have no business being in the building, being in breeches, being in the way!"

"I was all ready to turn aside, I swear. I was positive he'd keep going, and why shouldn't I be? *You* never yielded a jump to me in your life!"

"But he's a bloody gentleman, brat, and he thought you were a bloody lady!"

Things were going to get bloody indeed, Max thought, lying there in the sawdust. He levered himself up as best he could and shouted, "Halt!" in tones that had been heard over enemy cannons. Max had never stuttered during battle yet. The grooms who were running toward them stopped in their tracks. Even Atlas stopped his mad gallop. White-faced, Evan sank to his knees beside Max. On his other side, Merry did the same, only tears were running down her cheeks.

"I am fine," Max lied, knowing the pain would start in seconds. He was determined to make himself understood first, before he passed out, which, he sincerely hoped, would be before Jake or the local sawbones tried to set his leg. He looked at Evan first. "Don't you ever, ever speak to a lady that way again. Especially not this lady."

Evan nodded, biting his lip, so Max turned to Merry. He wished he could offer her his handkerchief. "Don't cry, my lady. You were not at fault. I wasn't paying attention, is that clear?"

He looked at both of them and Jake, who was feeling his limbs for breaks. "Lady Merry is not to be blamed. Tell Lord Carroll I said—"

Chapter Twenty-one

$\mathcal{M}$erry was still crying at Max's side when he awoke. Lud, was he still in the sawdust? He'd hoped, when the blackness overcame him, to have the worst of it over when he came to, the worst being Merry's heartrending sobs. He focused on his surroundings and discovered he was in a bed that was not in his room at the Manor. They must have carried him to one of the guest chambers at Winterpark. He couldn't feel his leg, which experience told him meant he was drugged. So the doctor must have come and gone, thank goodness. Now all he had to worry about was Merry's misery. "It was not your fault," Max whispered through dry lips. "Please don't cry." At least the laudanum had relaxed his tongue enough for him to speak without hesitation.

Merry jumped up and grabbed for his hand, jostling the bed. Now he could feel his leg. "I'm so sorry," she wailed. "I'll never forgive myself. Please, please get better. Oh, Max, say you're not mad at me. I couldn't bear it if you hated me."

Max didn't answer, having slipped back into blessed unconsciousness.

The next time he awoke, he had to go through the entire scenario: a weeping woman, a strange bed, "Don't cry." This time he was able to pay more attention to his surroundings. "Lud, this is a gentleman's bedroom, Lady Merry. You shouldn't be here!"

"The door is open, and Mama says it's all right. Miss Krupp, the duchess's companion, offered to sit here, too, for propriety." The duchess had actually done the offering, sending Miss Krupp to make sure the ragtag female didn't cause any more rumpus and riot.

Miss Krupp? Max groaned, and not because he was in pain. Then he looked around. The only chaperon he could find was Merry's dog, Downsy.

Merry just hunched her shoulders. "Miss Krupp doesn't like dogs. But it doesn't matter, there's no one else to help sit with you during the day, this close to the wedding. One of the footmen will be on call to look after your needs, but Mama says I'm useless for anything else anyway, and I'm not fit to be seen by company. She doesn't want Downsy downstairs either."

Max could understand Lady Carroll's decision. Merry's eyes were all red and swollen, and the dog was an undisciplined lummox. "Still, I don't want to be a burden. With all the guests . . ."

"No, it's no bother, really. Evan wanted to take you home to the Manor, but Papa and Bartholemew thought you'd do better here. Two of Comfort's friends were officers home on leave, so Evan took them to Blakely Manor so you could have their room instead. Evan's in alt, as you can imagine, although he's not talking to me."

"I'll tell him again that it wasn't your fault."

"He thinks it scandalous that I was wearing breeches. Mama made me burn them."

"That's too bad. I thought they were . . . pretty. You looked fine in them, and you rode like . . . like an angel." Max wasn't used to paying pretty compliments. That was the best he could do, after falling off his horse for her. His laudanum-laced words must have been the right ones, though, and well enough spoken, for her tears stopped.

"Oh, Max, do you think so? Do you mind if I call you Max? Then you can call me Merry. I *told* them you didn't stutter. Do you want some lemonade? Broth? Cook brewed some willow-bark tea. Do you have the headache, too?"

He would soon. "Sh, Merry. You don't have to fuss. It's only a broken leg. I've had worse."

Max had had a lot worse, in field hospitals, medical tents, and casualty ships. Here his every need was met, most of them by the most darling girl this side of heaven. Merry brought him food and drinks and cool cloths for his head. She read to him about raising cows. Whoever did that for him on the officers' ward?

Miss Krupp poked her bony nose into the room at odd moments, sniffed for signs of depravity and dog, then left. The footman made sure Max lacked for nothing, and Evan came often, with dice and cards and the other army officers.

Even when he was alone, though, when he could hear the faint sounds of music and laughter from the happy gatherings downstairs, Max was at peace. Later, after they had all gone home or to bed, he still felt content. He studied his books and dreamed of making his farm a success. It would never equal Winterpark, naturally, but it would make a decent living. When it did, in a few years, he'd come back to Berkshire and ask Lord Carroll for his daughter's hand. The earl would likely laugh at his presumptuousness, but Max would try anyway. Of course, Merry was sure to get snabbled up as soon as she made her formal bows to Society. She'd be claimed by an aristocrat with a real title to his name, a real estate instead of a few acres of land, and a real fortune. Certes he'd have a smooth tongue, without benefit of laudanum.

Max hoped the flash cove would love and appreciate Merry as she deserved. As he would, were she his.

"I do not like the situation one bit, Bradford. The child will not leave the lieutenant's sickroom. Some of the other guests are beginning to whisper among themselves. And that Almira Krupp is no help as a chaperon, for heaven knows where she is half the time."

Lord Carroll was trying to massage some of the tension out of his wife's neck and shoulders. Now he tried to relieve her mind: "Don't worry about Merry, Bess. Nothing can happen with Grey's leg in that huge cast. Let her ease her conscience by sitting with him. Missy won't pull such tricks again, I assure you."

The countess was nearly purring under her husband's stroking fingers. "I suppose. And she is being pushed aside by all the wedding to-do."

"And the lad did us a service by not strangling her, so we owe him more congenial company than the footman and that pinch-faced prude. Besides, Max is good practice for when you take our girl to London. With a little Town bronze, she'll be snapped up before the cat can lick its ear."

"I thought we'd agreed she was too young."

"She is, but if an eligible *parti* should happen on the scene and Merry were willing, I wouldn't say no."

The countess turned, out of reach of his touch. The purring changed to the snarl of a tigress defending her cubs. "You shall not, Bradford, rush Meredyth into any ill-advised, ill-planned marriage."

"Now, Bess," he soothed. "You know you are happy with Comfort and Rendell for the other girls, despite the hurry to get them shackled."

"But I am not in a hurry to push my last child, my baby, out of the nest."

"Well, I've been thinking about that, too, how you're going to miss having the youngsters about. Wouldn't it be nice, when all the girls have married and gone their own ways, to have a child around the house again?"

What child? Bess wondered, but she did not want to ask, to find out. "We shall have grandchildren soon enough." She stood and gathered up her stack of papers from the table next to the sofa. "It's growing late. I must look over the gardener's list again, of what foliage he thinks will be usable for the church."

"I'm sure the decision between holly and mistletoe can wait till tomorrow," the earl urged with sinking hopes as his beloved Bess walked toward her bedchamber door.

"It could, Bradford, if I had a year to plan the wedding, or even six months. But you had to get your two elder daughters married off before the New Year, for your own devious purposes, I don't doubt."

And Lord Carroll didn't doubt he'd be sleeping alone again tonight.

Since there was no fever, Dr. Petkin allowed as how Max could be carried downstairs so he didn't miss all of the festivities. Miss the disapproving duchess, the prinked and prissy peahens giggling in corners, or the local louts hovering over Merry? He'd rather have her to himself, thank you.

Down he went, willy-nilly, carried in a chair by Evan, the footman, and the two officers whose room he'd usurped, under Bartholemew's supervision.

Winterpark had been transformed, right down to the mixed scents of cinnamon and cloves and evergreens that greeted Max at the bottom of the stairs. Yew branches and holly were everywhere, with red bows and colored candles scattered throughout. There were swagged garlands at the windows and mantels and banister railings, and intricately woven balls of vines and mistletoe hanging over every door.

"Now, how did that get there, I wonder?" Lady Carroll pretended, to everyone's delight, as first her husband and then her new sons-in-law kissed her in the entryway to the drawing room. Every lady who entered—except the disapproving duchess and her critical companion—was kissed by the nearest or quickest male, or the one considered most formidable, such as Holly's or Joia's fiancé when it was their turn. Lord Carroll made sure he got a kiss from each of his girls, declaring this his favorite part of Christmas. Except for the wassail or the carols or the decorations.

"Oh, Papa!" three voices chimed together.

Merry had come in, and Evan, closest to the door, kissed her cheek. "Peace on earth, brat. Friends?"

She gazed back at him so adoringly that Max felt his stomach lurch. When one of the officers hurried to catch her under the kissing bough, Max knew he was going to be sick. He watched, though, as Merry ducked around the next daring young man and, blushing, sped over to the chair next to Max. She gave him a grin. All was well.

Until Lord Carroll started asking everyone to tell about his or her favorite Christmas. Lud, Max thought, and he hadn't had any laudanum for two days. There were stories of getting a first pony, or the Christmas when so much snow fell that they delivered all the tenants' gifts by sleigh. Rendell told of a candlelit procession on skis down a Swiss Alp. Lady Carroll remembered her first Christmas at Winterpark, already knowing she was to bear the next generation of Carrolls. The earl chuckled at himself. "I love each and every one of them, by George. I'd never be able to pick."

Merry said her favorite Christmas was the last one, because they got better and better. Then everyone looked at Max. His uncles hadn't celebrated Christmas beyond church services and a goose for dinner, perhaps handing him a shilling. In the army, sometimes it was hard to tell which day was Christmas. He looked around at the friendly faces, especially one green-eyed one with a scattering of freckles, and said, "This one."

"Well spoken, my boy, well spoken." Lord Carroll was beaming, making sure everyone had a full cup of lamb's-wool punch. "A toast, to this Christmas. May it be everyone's merriest ever."

After more toasts to the wedding couples, to the earl and the countess, to the king and Lord Wellington, Evan jumped up. "I say, poor Max didn't get to kiss any of the ladies! We can't have that!" Before Max could tell him to stubble it, Evan had snagged a twig of mistletoe from the doorway and was holding it over Max's red-haired and red-faced head. If he could have gotten out of his chair, he'd have turned tail and run.

Ever the gracious hostess, Lady Carroll stepped forward to put him out of his embarrassed misery. "Merry Christmas, Sir Maxwell," she said, touching him lightly on the forehead. At her nod, Joia and Holly each kissed his cheek. One of the Ellingsworth cousins dashed over and smacked him on the lips, to Evan's glee. Max vowed to shoot the clunch and save the frogs the effort.

Then Merry kissed him. On the mouth. He didn't hear Evan's snickers about tomboys, or the countess's indrawn breath, or the duchess's cluck of condemnation. He just heard Merry's sigh. No Christmas carol ever sounded so sweet, no

Yuletide aromas ever smelled as enticing as her flowered scent, no wassail ever tasted as delicious as her lips. "M-merry Christmas, Merry."

"It must be time for Sir Maxwell to return to his bed," Lady Carroll declared. "He shouldn't do too much his first day out. Craighton, will you assist Evan and Lieutenant Smythe? Bartholemew, please send the footman. Bartholemew? Now, where has he gone off to?"

Max was duly restored to his chamber and assisted into his nightshirt, not regretting one whit that the party was continuing without him. He had his Christmas dream to cherish.

He was almost asleep when he heard voices in the corridor outside that meant some of the others were seeking their beds. Then his door opened. "Yes?" he called. "Who is there?"

" 'Tis I, Merry. I just wanted to make sure you hadn't over-done. Shall I mix you a dose of laudanum?"

The candle she carried revealed her concern. It also revealed that she was already in her nightclothes. Her feet were bare. "L-lud, Merry. You hadn't ought to be here."

She pointed to the dog at her side. "Downsy had to go out, so I thought I would check on you. I'm not staying or anything."

Downsy had other ideas. He'd been locked in Merry's bed-room all evening with only a pair of slippers to chew on. He did not want to be herded back there or, worse, out to the stables. So he dove under the bed. Merry set the candle down and bent to coax him out, giving Max a charming posterior view. Downsy ran out the other side of the bed and around the room, enjoying himself hugely now that he'd gotten his mis-tress to chase him.

"I've got you cornered now, you wretched beast," she laughed, lunging at the big dog. Downsy leaped out of her grasp, onto the bed. Onto Max's broken leg, in fact. He groaned.

"Oh, Max, are you all right?" Merry reached over to remove the hairy menace, but misbalanced and landed on the bed her-self. On Max's chest, in fact. He groaned.

"Oh, dear. I really am a catastrophe, aren't I?"

"You're perfect, Merry-mine." They were nose to nose, eye to eye. There was nothing for it but for Max to kiss her.

Which was when Miss Almira Krupp went by in the corridor. Seeing the young man's door open, she entered, to find the youngest daughter of the house, skirts above her knees, feet bare, in the embrace of a penniless soldier. She shrieked. Then she shrieked louder, so no one would wonder what she was doing headed to the duke's chambers instead of the duchess's.

The earl came running from belowstairs with Rendell, pistol in hand. Joia and Holly and Comfort and the duke all poured into the corridor, with half the Ellingsworths and hordes of servants. Lady Carroll arrived and added her cry of dismay to the scene.

Hearing the uproar, seeing the pistol, Max first thought to protect the treasure in his arms by throwing himself on top of her, as he would a fallen comrade. He had to be satisfied with holding her tighter, against his side.

"I told you the chit was a harum-scarum hussy," the Duchess of Carlisle announced from the foot of the bed, where she'd pushed her way through. "You'll have to get her married off on the instant. Too bad the boy is such a commoner, but no one else will ever take her after this night."

"But they're just children," Lady Carroll moaned, clutching her husband's arm.

He was shaking his head. "No keeping this mum, not with the audience. I'm sorry, my love, they'll have to be wed, and soon."

"How soon?" she cried.

"Quickly, else she'll be ruined for sure."

"I still have the special license," Rendell volunteered. "Holly and I had time for the banns to be read, so we never needed it. Sir Max could join us other benedicts on Christmas day."

"No," Lady Carroll wailed.

Lord Carroll was rubbing his chin. "What do you think, Max?"

"That I'd be the h-happiest of m-men if you g-gave me your d-d-daughter's h-hand in—"

Merry couldn't wait. She threw herself back onto his chest. "Oh, Max, me, too!"

While Bartholemew went to fetch the champagne, horrified that he hadn't been better prepared, everyone was laughing about how they were to get Max to the church and the ceremony, how Downsy would be best man, and how they were to keep Merry out of Max's bedroom until then. One person wasn't laughing. Lady Carroll was sobbing and beating her fists against her husband's chest.

PART FOUR

Adeste Infidelis

Chapter Twenty-two

A hundred weddings of note might have taken place at Saint George's, Hanover Square, that year, nay, a hundred and fifty. None was more memorable than the ceremony late that Christmas morning at little Saint Cecilia's in Carrolton village. What other tonnish affair could boast three exquisite women, three exceptional gentlemen including an heir to a dukedom, a man of fortune, and a hero, and three magnificent, well-run weddings in one? Mothers of marriage-aged daughters were filled with admiration. Fathers of marriage-aged daughters were filled with awe. Surely the wedding day of the Earl of Carroll's daughters would live on as a testament to good taste, good planning, and good luck. Pity the poor souls who weren't invited, or who were obliged to spend the holidays among their own kin. They'd only hear at secondhand or read in every newspaper how stunning an occasion it was.

The church was decorated in evergreens, white ribbons, and red roses from the length of England. Every conservatory and succession house in two counties was called on to contribute. The villagers and tenants lined the streets outside, all wearing their Sunday best, with sprigs of holly in their buttonholes or red ribbons in their hair. They cheered with sincere affection as Lady Carroll arrived, escorted by the Duke of Carlisle, and then the earl, in his streamer-strewn carriage, with his three daughters. Even the horses were decked out in ribbons and roses, and Jem Coachman, the footmen, and the outriders all had new green livery with red facings. The only one not matching was the tiny lad up next to the driver, in a too large coat and a knit cap pulled over his ears. Lady Carroll was already inside the church, however, so she didn't notice, and no one else cared if the coachman chose to bring his grandson or whatever along. The boy would have a memory to last for a lifetime.

So would Lord Carroll. The earl could scarce contain his happiness. This glorious day, in fact, was surpassed in his mind only by his own wedding, when he'd been too nervous to enjoy himself, too afraid that his Bess would change her mind at the last minute. But today he had nothing to worry about. All he had to do was smile—and hand his little girls into the keeping of strange men who would take them far away. He almost ordered Jem Coachman to turn the carriage around and return to Winterpark.

No, all nestlings had to fly away. The men waiting at the church, no doubt as anxiously as he'd done, were decent fellows. They weren't entirely worthy of his angels, but they'd do. Comfort was a bit rakish, but Joia would see he toed the line. Rendell was a tad old for Holly, but she'd be a wealthy widow if he shuffled off too soon. The marriage settlements were more than generous, they were lavish. The earl had seen to that. And the youngster, Sir Max, had bottom. He'd had to be carried to the coach, then wheeled into the chapel in a Bath chair, but he insisted on standing on his own two legs, one splinted and in a cast, for the ceremony. So there he was, freckles more noticeable in his pale face, waiting with the others at the altar for the first glimpse of his bride. He'd have a long wait, Lord Carroll feared, hoping the boy wouldn't keel over before Merry's turn. Evan stood by, a grinning best man for both Max and his father, just in case.

First the earl walked his eldest daughter down the aisle. Joia was dressed in white velvet and carried a bouquet of holly and red roses. Lord Carroll thought she was the most beautiful bride he'd ever seen, after her mother, of course. "I love you, precious," he told her before placing her hand in the viscount's. "I'll always love you."

Gouty foot and all, he walked back down the aisle, to where Holly and Merry were waiting in the vestibule in Bartholemew's capable care. Holly was wearing a dark red gown with a white lace overskirt, and she glowed. She was definitely the most beautiful bride in the world, after her mother. "Don't stay away too long, poppet. I want to see my grandchildren at Rendell Hall."

Then it was back for Merry, who placed a quick kiss on the old butler's lined cheek before placing her hand on her father's arm. Merry was dressed in green velvet that matched her sparkling eyes, with the hastily added white lace train from her mother's wedding gown. Was this his little tomboy in breeches? She was gorgeous, almost as beautiful as her mother had been. "I have big plans for that boy, mitten," the earl told her as they walked toward her waiting groom, standing tall and proud in his dress uniform.

"He's a man, Papa," Merry answered, "all the man I'll ever want."

The earl swallowed past the lump in his throat. He hoped the clunch could say his vows sometime today so they could get home in time for the wedding breakfast and the ball later.

Max's I-dos were loud and clear, to everyone's relief. Lord Carroll hadn't realized he'd been holding his breath, just as he hadn't realized he'd been weeping until a tear rolled down his chin. His Bess was sniffling beside him throughout the entire ceremony. Bradford hoped she had her own handkerchief for once, because he needed his.

The weddings concluded without a hitch. Max didn't fall on his face, no one was blinded by the diamond Rendell placed on Holly's finger, and the duke, standing as best man for his son, didn't pinch any of the choir members. Afterward, they all got into gaily decorated carriages for the ride to Winterpark. Bess was wiping her eyes, so didn't notice the extra passenger riding up with the driver.

The breakfast was as lavish as one expected at Winterpark, and continued without pause straight into the ballroom. Another orchestra, another feast, was set up in the indoor riding arena for servants and tenants, with the brides and grooms eating, drinking, and dancing at both parties. Then they were off, all of them.

Comfort and Joia were going to Austria on a diplomatic mission, Holly and Rendell on business, and Merry and Max simply on honeymoon. Everyone thought that would be best, so there would be less unpleasant speculation about Merry's hurried wedding. Max couldn't do anything about his farm until spring, anyway, until his leg healed. Lord Carroll was sure a broken leg wouldn't interfere with the boy's enjoyment of Rendell's yacht or Comfort's leased chalet—or his new bride.

All in all, Lord Carroll was more than content as he shook the last guest's hand and shared a final toast with his butler. Of course, he'd prefer his girls closer, but they'd be back, perhaps with children of their own. And they'd be well cherished, he knew, by the men they loved. What more could a father want for his little girls? The earl would be thoroughly delighted now, if only Bess weren't so distraught.

"What's wrong, my love? Are you still missing the girls?" The earl pulled his wife closer to him on the sofa in their sitting room. He'd been busier than ever, overseeing the shipping of Comfort's horses and the renovations at Rendell Hall. Bess was still wandering aimlessly around Winterpark. Lord Carroll was worried. "It's been a month and we get letters from one or t'other nearly every day. Did Merry ever have a governess, by the way? I recall paying an exorbitant salary to some nondescript woman with a bun, but you'd never know it from mitten's spelling."

"Of course she did, Bradford, all of my daughters were well educated. But you kept letting Meredyth escape the schoolroom to follow you about Winterpark like a puppy, so you have no one to blame but yourself."

"Speaking of that, you didn't lose a daughter, you got rid of that impossible mutt. I don't know what possessed the chit to drag a half-trained mongrel along with them."

"Perhaps your threatening to drown the dog if Downsy

chewed another one of your gloves," his wife answered with a smile that didn't quite reach her eyes and faded quickly.

"Mitten knew I'd never harm the pup. I can't tell from her latest letter whether he raised his leg on a Mongol prince or he raided the pantry for a leg of mutton. Then again, Holly's letters are so interspersed with German, I need my old grammar books. I don't know what I'll do when she starts spouting Russian, from her new studies."

"You don't think they'll go there next, do you? It's so far away." Bess dabbed at her eyes.

She seemed to be crying all the time, the earl fretted, stroking her shoulder. "Not so far away from where they are now, my love. But they promised to return for Christmas next year at Rendell Hall. And Joia's news is good—in a clear hand, too—that Comfort thinks we'll have peace at last."

"Praise heaven, it should be soon."

"Aye, then Joia and the viscount will be home, and they promised to make a nice long stay on their way to Ireland. The only one who will regret the end of war is young Rendell, and I'm sure he'll find some rowdydow, now that he's had a taste of battle."

"I never thought I'd miss him, but I do."

"You know, Bess, maybe we should go to London. Winterpark is too empty and you're too sad. You could go shopping, take in the opera or the theater, visit some of your old friends."

"No one is there this time of year."

"Then what about Bath? Perhaps the waters will be good for my foot."

"You've refused to drink the nasty stuff every time we've gone. Besides, the Duchess of Carlisle is there, and we just got rid of the old harridan, Bradford. I don't know if I could be civil through one more iteration of Meredyth's fall from Her Grace's grace."

Lord Carroll was determined to find something to bring his beloved out of the blue devils. "Then what say we go to Austria? Everyone is there, including our girls. They say it's the most glittering assembly Europe has ever seen."

She raised hopeful eyes to his for a moment, then lowered

her gaze to the handkerchief clenched in her hands. "No, we cannot intrude on their honeymoons. No one needs their in-laws around at a time like that." She blew her nose. "No one needs me at all."

"Ah, Bess, I need you. You are the stuff that holds my world together, don't you know?"

"What, am I glue, then? You always did have a way with words, my dear." At least she smiled. "No, let the children enjoy themselves. Besides, I know how you hate to travel, Bradford."

"But I hate more to see you unhappy, my love. We could stay in a hotel of our own, see the sights by ourselves. Like another honeymoon for us, don't you know. Then we can bring Merry and Max back with us, help them get settled in their new place. I have plans for that young man, Bess, if he learns as quickly as I think he will. I'm hoping he'll take over running this place in a few years, and oversee Rendell's property for him as well. Maybe Evan's, if the lad doesn't get home soon. It will be a good life for them, just what Merry will enjoy the most, and she'll be close by, too."

Bess heeded only one sentence. "You manage Winterpark, Bradford, and always shall."

"Not forever, my dear. I'm already relying more and more on bailiffs and agents. That's not like one of the family. I have to prepare for the future, my love, for your future."

"Oliver will own Winterpark, Bradford," she noted with a lack of enthusiasm. "He'll pick his own estate managers and advisers."

"That's another reason we should go to Vienna. Do you realize that not one letter from the girls mentions Oliver? I'd like to know what he's up to. No, my love, I shall not leave you to Oliver's mercy. Can you see Aubergine Willenborg taking on your duties as mistress here, visiting the sick, keeping the still room, administering the village school?"

"Well, I shan't stay to see it, Bradford. I'll get a cottage of my own and travel from daughter to daughter, visiting my grandchildren."

"As Oliver's pensioner, like that Almira Krupp female?"

"What, my lord, do you not intend to leave me better provided for than that? Shall I be saving my pin money?" Bess knew her husband was the most generous of men. "Perhaps I'd better start lining my pockets from the household accounts."

"You know you'll never want for anything as long as I live, dearest, or after I'm gone."

"Don't speak that way, Bradford. I don't care how wealthy I am as a widow."

"I have to speak of it, Bess, because you'll still have to deal with Oliver. He'll go through his wife's money in no time. Then he'll destroy everything we've built, our family's heritage. You know he cares nothing for the land. Not even Merry and Max can protect Winterpark when I am gone."

Now it was the countess's turn to offer solace. "There is no other option, my dear, so stop fretting. I cannot be happy with the thought of Aubergine standing as chatelaine in my place, but I shan't be happy without you, no matter what or where. Oliver cannot keep the dower house from me, so I'll be here to make sure he doesn't pillage the estate. I owe you that, for not bearing you a son."

"Oh, Bess, no—"

"Yes, and I have regretted it my whole life, especially knowing how you feel about your cousin's child. But there is no choice."

"What if there is a choice, Bess? What if we have a chance to bring love and laughter back into this great rambling barn of a place that's so empty without the girls? What if I found a way to safeguard everything I hold dear?" He rocked her close to him, telling her without words that she was the dearest.

"What, would you conjure a different successor out of thin air?"

"No, out of Sussex." Bess stiffened and would have moved out of the earl's arms altogether, but he wouldn't let her. "No, this time you have to hear me out, Bess. There is a boy, my love, you know there is. If I were to legally adopt him, give him my name . . ."

"What, you expect me to welcome your bast—your by-blow, your—"

"Son." He stated it quietly but firmly.

"Your son," Bess repeated. "Your illegitimate son. You want me to bring him into our home, where everyone would know how you betrayed me? That's why you wanted the girls out of the house so fast, wasn't it? So they couldn't criticize their idol, their dear papa. That's why you pushed Evan at Hollice, so she'd take Rendell, and why you left Meredyth alone with that soldier until the inevitable happened. You wanted them gone," she angrily accused, "so you could bring your baseborn child here without their censure."

Lord Carroll could not deny her charges. "I thought you would accept the boy more readily without the girls' reputations to think of, and I would not bring unwanted gossip to their come-outs."

"No," she countered bitterly, "you'd only bring scandal into my own parlor. Well, you are wrong, sir, I shall not accept another woman's child. Oliver would only challenge you through the courts, anyway, creating more of a bumblebroth."

"Oliver won't be a problem. He knows I can have him up on charges in an instant. An English lord can beat his wife or renege on his tailor's bills. He cannot cheat at cards. Besides, I have all those extra titles floating around. I'll make him a viscount or something and offer him a generous allowance. That should satisfy him and that harpy he married. Listen, Bess, I have checked with my solicitors. It's been done. If I—if we—adopt the boy, the law would have to recognize his right. We could give out that he was my brother Jack's grandson, so there'd be less talk."

"Your brother died without issue. Everyone knows that."

"No, they only know that he didn't have an English wife and children. Besides, I am an earl. Do you think anyone is going to disagree to my face if I say the boy is a product of Jack's short, secret French marriage? No one will, especially not with Rendell to guard his finances and Comfort to see him established in society and Max Grey to oversee his properties. You'd be his guardian with them, to guide him, to raise him into the man I'd want. Winterpark needs you here forever. And I need you with me on this."

"What of my needs, my home and family, my husband's loyalty?"

"You've got it, dash it. One night out of twenty-one years, Bess, that's all it was."

That's all? It was a stake through her heart. Lady Carroll stood. "You know, perhaps a jaunt to Austria might be pleasant. You're right, I've been pining over the girls too much."

"Don't do this to me, Bess," the earl begged, but his Bess was already on the other side of a very closed door.

Chapter Twenty-three

*Th*e food was too rich in Vienna, the social rounds were too hectic, and Bess was too busy to spend time alone with her husband. She planned it that way, Lord Carroll knew, and he hated every minute of the trip, except when he was with one or the other of his daughters.

Joia was already becoming a political hostess of note, and Holly had begun a literary salon. Merry was the darling of the military set, with Max a quiet, smiling presence at her side. Each was a success, but more important, each one's marriage was a success. All three happy couples wanted to show the Carrolls the sights, entertain them in style, and introduce them to the cream of Viennese society.

There was too much blasted cream, Lord Carroll grumbled. He was growing fat on flawn, and his gout was worse than ever. He was expected to dress up and waltz every damn night besides, like a trained pony at Astley's Amphitheatre. Of course, he was gratified the gentlemen he'd selected for his daughters were proving so satisfactory, but now that he'd seen that for himself, the earl wanted to go home.

Bess, on the other hand, seemed determined to take in every overcrowded party, visit every boring museum and suffocating gallery, listen to every pluck of every blasted violin string. Between times the countess shopped with the girls to round out their incomplete trousseaux and so she'd have something to wear to all the events. Not only was Lord Carroll deprived of his wife's companionship, but he was paying handsomely for the privilege. No, he was paying for his past sins, and well he knew it. By the time they finally retired at night, Bess was too exhausted to talk, of course.

His dear wife was trying to avoid his presence, Bradford believed, so that he couldn't press her about the succession, as if, by ignoring the issue, she could make it disappear. Instead, with every ball and breakfast, Carroll was more convinced that he was too old for all this claptrap, that he should get his house in order before it was too late.

So he went looking for Oliver.

His hapless heir wasn't in attendance at any of the court functions, nor any of the sporting events, coffeehouses, or gambling establishments. None of the girls had seen their cousin or his wife, either. Lord Carroll was able to track them down finally, but only through Joia's husband's contacts at the Consulate. Sons-in-law were handy for something, even if they couldn't purchase their own wives' bride clothes.

The address the earl had been given was in an unfashionable outskirt of Vienna, where few of the foreign tourists bothered to visit. The earl was happy he'd brushed up on his schoolboy German. He was also happy he'd thought to change his blunt into local currency. Oliver's landlady, it appeared, was not about to permit him to visit the sapskull until Oliver's rent was paid, plus bills for his medicine, doctor, and food.

The once-dandified Oliver was a sorry mess, and Lord Carroll was never sorrier he was connected to the makebate after he'd heard Oliver's tale of woe.

Aubergine, it seemed, regretted her bargain within days of the hasty marriage. The Tulip's shirt points were the only stiff thing about him, the earl surmised from Oliver's garbled account. As soon as they got to Vienna and the new Mrs. Carroll realized that she was even less socially acceptable than before, that Oliver's expectations could not gain her entry into the *haut monde*, she'd been more displeased. She didn't speak the language, not even French, didn't have a single acquaintance among the English elite, and didn't want to waste her brass paying the inept wastrel's gambling debts. So she'd decamped with a Polish count and Lord Carroll's wedding gift money.

Oliver hadn't been able to satisfy his obligations, not even the Austrian boot-maker who, unlike the English tradesmen, actually demanded payment on delivery. The fop knew he couldn't send to his cousin for more funds, Lord Carroll having made that clear on the occasion of signing the wedding check. So Oliver went to a moneylender. When he found that his luck hadn't turned, that he couldn't repay this new, higher-rate-of-interest creditor, Oliver did what he usually did: he cheated at cards. And what happened was what usually happened: he got caught. This time the flat he'd chosen to fleece was a Prussian major who called him out, then laid him out with a bullet in the shoulder. Which still didn't get Oliver's debts to the cents-percenter paid. That displeasured businessman sent an associate to beat Oliver to a pulp, saying he'd kill him in a fortnight if the money was not forthcoming.

And that, Oliver concluded, was why he was hiding out in a run-down room with a lamprey for a landlady, both eyes swollen shut, half his teeth missing, and his dealing arm in a sling. He'd take any offer his cousin was willing to make if it would get him out of this benighted country alive. An allowance, a minor title, *and* a plantation in Jamaica? Where should he sign his disclaimer to the succession? Oliver would endorse it without looking, with his left hand. Hell, he'd use his own blood if the landlady wouldn't provide ink.

Sons-in-law were deuced convenient indeed, Lord Carroll congratulated himself. Rendell's people handled the settlement with the moneylender, Comfort's connections made the travel arrangements, and Max's departing army friends acted as escort to ensure Oliver got on his ship. Of course, all three of the girls' husbands were happy to get their cousin-by-marriage, clunch-by-birth, out of the country and out of their lives. They weren't as happy as Lord Carroll, however. Bess was ready to go home.

Merry and Max were anxious to take up the reins of their own property. They invited the earl and countess to come along to Kent, to offer advice and suggestions toward making the farm profitable, the house livable. Merry could have managed the place with her eyes closed, but she was wise enough to let Max do the deciding. Merry was good for the lad, and his quiet calm was good for her. They didn't need their in-laws hanging about.

Not even Bess could think of an excuse to linger in Kent, especially not with Joia and Comfort expected back in England soon. The countess was planning to meet their arrival in London to save them the extra travel time, and stay on there until they left for Ireland. Meantime, she threw herself into a frenzy of housekeeping at Winterpark, changing the girls' bedrooms into suites for when they came to visit with their husbands. She also supervised an addition to the village school, a total refurbishment of Saint Cecilia's, and the construction of a new infirmary. B'gad, her husband lamented, she'd see to paving the roads next, rather than spend time with him.

The earl and countess seldom visited in their sitting room anymore. Both found it too painful to look at the hurt in the other's eyes. Bess felt betrayed by Bradford's demands; Lord Carroll felt betrayed by his wife's distrust. She wouldn't listen to him, much less see his viewpoint. For the first time in over twenty years, there was a coldness in the air at Winterpark, a palpable feeling that each would rather be somewhere else, with someone else.

Carroll thought he might not go to London when Bess went. She'd enjoy herself more without his crotchets and complaints. And why should he suffer the fools in Town, when he could suffer just as well in the country? It wasn't as if Bess was going to share his bedroom there, any more than she was sharing his concerns here.

The earl slammed his fist down on the breakfast table. No, by George, he was not going to spend what time he had left on God's green earth breathing soot in the city. And he was not going to live every day paying for one night of insobriety. "Bess," he shouted across the long table, "do you still love me?"

Bartholemew cleared his throat, then he cleared the room of himself and the two footmen carrying trays to the sideboard.

Bess couldn't claim exhaustion or a busy schedule, so she

tried a diversion. "What a lovely display you put on for the servants, my lord."

"I do not care one whit about the servants' opinions. I want to know if you still love me."

Very much on her uppers, the countess replied, "Of course I do, but that doesn't mean I don't think you are a fool."

"Fine," he countered. "I love you, too, albeit I think you are as stubborn as a jackass."

"Good, we're agreed on something." She sipped her tea.

The earl stood and gestured at the long stretch of mahogany between them. "Will you meet me halfway, Bess? Please, my dear?"

Since the countess had been as wretched as her lord, she nodded, knowing he didn't merely mean the table. Carrying her cup and plate to where he was now standing midpoint, the countess took the chair opposite the earl's.

He waited until she was seated. "The Barlowes are leaving for America before summer."

"Since I neither know anyone named Barlowe nor have any interest in them, I'm sure I wish them good luck and good riddance."

"The Barlowes are the people who have been taking care of the boy." The earl knew he didn't have to mention which boy. "They have two sons and a girl of their own they want to see make their way in the New World. I can't let the boy go."

"You let your daughters go."

"That was different, Bess. The girls were ready and I knew someone would look after them as well as I would. The boy has nobody."

"Bradford, we've been through all this. I cannot accept your natural son in my home. Send him off to school if you can't bear the idea of his finding a new life for himself, too."

"He's already in school, Bess. But what about long vacations and holidays? Is he to have no home, nowhere to go, no one to care for him at all?"

Bess's heart melted a little at the thought of some poor waif left behind when the other boys went home for the summer.

But he wasn't *her* responsibility. "Do not try to enlist my sympathy, Bradford, for it will not work. He is another woman's child. Let her take him in."

Lord Carroll reached over the table and took her hand, feeling better for the simple contact. "She's dead, my dear, from an influenza epidemic at the school where she taught. I don't know if she ever saw the boy after his birth. I doubt it. I do swear on my life that I never saw the woman again. Agents handled everything, her lease, her expenses."

Lady Carroll nodded her acceptance of the earl's avowal. He'd not lie about a thing like that. He hadn't even lied about the first time, when she'd wished he had. "What kind of unnatural mother— No, that is none of my affair. Besides, a woman like that, no better than she ought to be, why, you cannot even be certain the child is yours."

The earl let go of her hand and sipped at his coffee, a smile on his face. "Do you remember Merry as a tot, how we used to tease that she was an Irish leprechaun switched in the crib for our own blue-eyed, blond-haired infant?"

The countess's features softened, too. "She was all red curls and big green eyes and freckles. You used to say the fairies left her on our doorstep for good luck. And she was as bright and shining as a lucky ha'penny, wasn't she?"

"Aye, and always smiling, even when she had no teeth. I swear she was my favorite of all the girls."

"You never had a favorite in your life, Bradford Carroll. You had enough love for every one of your children."

"And for one more, Bess. For one more." He took a miniature out of his pocket and handed it across the table.

Bess studied the portrait of a grinning boy, with those same red curls and green eyes. "I'd forgotten Meredyth had those oversized ears of yours, too, Bradford." To this day, the earl wore his silver hair cut long over his ears, hair that had been the same vibrant auburn when she first met him. "I swear I thought she would never grow into them, and I was never so relieved as when short curls became all the crack."

"That's not my portrait, Bess. It's the boy's."

The countess sat back in her chair. There was no question of the child's paternity, then. Speaking of butter-stamps, the boy could have had the family's coat of arms tattooed on his forehead and been less conspicuously a Carroll.

"You see?" the earl asked. "People will accept him as my brother Jack's grandson."

"They will *never* accept him, Bradford. Stop dreaming."

"They will if you do. If we give him our name, take him into our home, how can anyone question us? The Duke of Carlisle will sponsor him. Damn, I'll get Rendell to whisper in Prinny's ear. We can make it work, Bess. And he's a fine boy, bright and well mannered. You'll like him."

"What, you've seen him?" The countess felt betrayed all over again. The child was no longer a faceless entity existing in limbo; now he was a real boy, stealing her husband's affection from her own children, from her.

"I had to, to make sure he was healthy and not in need of anything."

"And what if I need you to leave this be, to let him go to America with a decent family, one he knows?"

"Don't make me choose, Bess, I beg of you."

"I am your wife, Bradford. Your legal wife who has borne you three beautiful children who bear your name. There should be no choice."

Chapter Twenty-four

*N*othing was settled, yet both the earl and his countess were resolved to stop the conflict. Pain for one meant pain for the other; that was how they'd lived the last twenty-one years, and that was how they intended to keep living. The love they shared just had to be enough to see them through this muddle, too. Lord Carroll wouldn't press Bess about taking the boy into their home, and Lady Carroll wouldn't deny Bradford his son outside it. He hadn't given up, and she hadn't backed down.

Nothing more was said, but that night they clung together like young lovers reunited after a separation, holding tightly to each other after the lovemaking, as if to keep the world from intruding between them. It would in the morning, of course, but they could pretend.

The household was relieved that the master and mistress seemed to have reconciled their differences. Bartholemew just shook his head, seeing a temporary truce instead of a negotiated peace. He hoped the diplomats in Vienna were having better luck.

In March Lady Carroll went to London to welcome Joia and her husband home. Lord Carroll went along, reluctant but resigned, until he realized Comfort was escort enough for the ladies, and the viscount actually enjoyed the social rounds. The elegant aristocrat had to be the finest son-in-law a man could have, the earl decided.

Merry and Max joined them at Carroll House in Grosvenor

Square just before Comfort and Joia left for Ireland. With everything in hand at their cottage and Max's leg nearly healed, the countess insisted that Meredyth have her proper come-out. Having been denied the grand weddings of her dreams, Bess was determined to see her youngest daughter's presentation done in style, with hooped skirts, tiara, and fancy balls, all the ruffles and rigmarole of a debutante Season.

Merry made her bows at the queen's drawing room in April, but as Lady Grey, not Lady Meredyth Carroll, which, her fond parents agreed, was a fine thing for the family reputation since the irrepressible chit grinned through the whole affair, winked at Max, and had dog hair on her gloves. During the weeks of fittings and furbishings and feminine folderol, Max proved to be a solid bastion of male companionship for the earl, who was pleased to introduce the young hero around at his clubs. Max was a good listener, but more important, he was a conscientious property owner who wanted to get home to his piece of land. With Merry's hearty approval, her Season lasted all of two weeks. Bless the lad, Lord Carroll thought. Max had to be the world's best son-in-law.

In June, though, Lord and Lady Carroll received a letter from Holly, saying that she was expecting a blessed event in the New Year. Mr. Rendell instantly became the earl's favorite son-in-law.

Also in June, Lord Carroll took on a new groom, one of those fashionable new tigers. All the swells had boys riding behind their seats, the earl casually explained to his wife, to jump down and hold the horses. The boy was a relative of Jem Coachman, he said, and would only be at Winterpark for the summer, sleeping over the stable with the other grooms.

But the boy was too small and frail to hold Carroll's high-strung cattle. He wasn't dressed in livery, either, just an ill-fitting assortment of pants and shirts, with a knit cap pulled over his ears. And he didn't have to cling to any precarious perch, Bess noted from her bedroom window that overlooked the carriage drive. He sat on the bench next to her harebrained, ham-handed husband.

How could Bradford think she wouldn't know? Everyone

knew, she was sure, from the housekeeper's pursed lips to her abigail's sympathetic looks. Bartholemew avoided her altogether, a sure sign of divided loyalties. Well, let them pity her, Bess decided. Her husband was happy with his new plaything, like Meredyth with her mongrel pup, and Bradford's mongrel was going to stay in the stable where he belonged.

Bess's conscience declared war on her righteous indignation. He was just a child, her eyes and her heart told her, an innocent child hardly more than a babe. He was a motherless boy with the stigma of bastardy—who'd done absolutely nothing to deserve his fate. Life was hard, Bess forced herself to reply. Better he learn that lesson now.

What he was learning was the layout of Winterpark, as the earl took the boy with him on his visits to the tenant farmers and their families. He was learning to ride as well. Bess watched from her window as Bradford's little shadow followed him on a sleek and shiny pony. The girls had outgrown their ponies by their tenth birthdays; there hadn't been one in the stables in years. Perhaps life wasn't going to be so hard for the earl's natural son. Many men took responsibility for their by-blows, Lady Carroll acknowledged. They raised them and saw them settled in positions of respect. They just didn't make them their heirs. *Send him away,* Bess silently pleaded. *An' you love me, Bradford, send him away.*

The boy did leave in August, but the countess would not ask where. To school, another family, it mattered not, there was no constant, nagging reminder of the family's shame. He left in the earl's own carriage, his pony tied behind, like no stableboy Bess had ever seen. She didn't care. Her husband's bastard son was gone.

So was some of Bradford's happiness, though. He seemed to age overnight, requiring naps in the afternoon, complaining of his swollen joints and aching foot. At night now, it was the earl who claimed exhaustion when Bess would have shared his bed. By day, he spent less time with his beloved horses and more time with the estate books, shouting at the servants, complaining Cook's food was making him ill, telling Bartholemew he was not at home to callers, friends and neighbors alike.

"What about the hunt ball?" Bess wanted to know. "Are you too blue-deviled to hold the annual party? Will it be too much of a strain for you, all that company and entertaining?"

"Do what you will, madam. You always do."

The countess worried in truth now, for if Bradford was willing to forgo his cherished hunt and the huge house party that always went with it, he was ailing indeed, if only sore at heart. She wrote to Meredyth and Joia, asking them to come early for the visit and to stay longer. Hollice and Rendell were expected back before Christmas so their child could be born at Rendell Hall, but no date of arrival had been mentioned in their letters. Still, two out of three daughters ought to brighten Carroll's spirits, his wife firmly believed.

He was gladdened by the girls' acceptances, but more so, Bess was angry to realize, by the boy's return. She wouldn't have known he was back except that she saw the pony in one of the paddocks when she drove past on her way to visit a tenant family. That and Bradford's suddenly recovered interest in his horses, for he seldom left the barns anymore, the cad.

The child ought to be in school instead of dawdling around a stable yard, the countess told herself, where he'd be noticed immediately on her daughters' arrivals. They might be married now and know such things existed, but they did not need to know their own father's indiscretion in a knit cap.

She wouldn't ask, of course. Silent indifference and feigned ignorance seemed to be part of their unspoken pact. Nor would she lower herself to gossiping with the servants. Bartholemew, however, did not count.

"The young groom, Lord Carroll's tiger, is surely of an age to be at school, don't you think?" she asked the butler one afternoon, as though idly wondering why the child wasn't at classes in the village.

Looking past her shoulder, Bartholemew answered, "Quite, but there was a measles outbreak at the academy where he was enrolled." As if stable brats frequently attended boarding school. "They sent the boys home. The little chap is fine, though. Jake Groom is taking good care of him."

"I thought he was Jem Coachman's grandson, Bartholemew."

"Indeed, my lady. But Jake has, ah, more experience with boys."

Since neither Jem nor Jake had ever been married to her certain knowledge, Bess shook her head. "Get your stories straight, old man," she said, turning her back on Bartholemew's fumbling, annoyed that she couldn't demand the child's removal now. She'd thought of sending him to one of the cottagers—everyone must already know of his existence, the way Carroll trotted the boy around the countryside all summer—and to the village school, but she couldn't, not if the boy was ill or if he'd spread the disease to the local children.

The doctor was not sent for, so the boy must not be very sick, Bess told herself, angry that she was concerned despite her firmest intentions, irritated that she kept looking to see if the pony was out being ridden. She would *not* fret over Bradford's by-blow. He was another woman's son, not hers. Never hers.

Then Lord Carroll was called away. There had been heavy rain and floods in the north that autumn, and the earl's Yorkshire sheep farm was heavily damaged. Worse, his bailiff had caught an inflammation of the lungs out trying to save the flocks, so there was no one to order repairs or hire more workers. The earl had to go, and Bess had to stay, with the house party nearly upon them. The girls could arrive any time, along with the other hunt party guests, including Comfort's father, whom she'd been obliged to invite. The duchess had accepted an invitation for Christmas, to no one's gratification.

"Besides, my love, I'll make better time alone. You know you don't like sleeping in the carriage or driving through the night."

She didn't like the idea of his going without her either, not with the evidence of a previous solo journey residing over the stables. "Will you take your, ah, tiger with you?"

"No, the journey will be too hard." He touched her cheek and she bit her lip, reading the question in his eyes. She shook her head before he could say the words, so he asked, "Will you look in on my . . . horses, Bess?"

* * *

This was all a trick of Bradford's, the countess fumed, leaving her alone with that boy so she'd feel sorry for him, so she'd care for him. Well, she wouldn't. She inquired of Jake, when he brought her gig around for her to go on morning calls. The lad was improving, the head groom reported, though still too weak to ride.

Her children were never sickly, Bess gloated as she drove off alone, and immediately felt guilty. The countess was ashamed enough of her base thoughts that she decided to go check on the boy herself. What did men know about treating children? And it was not, she argued with her inner thoughts, as if the boy were an orphaned kitten that, once blanketed and bottle-fed, was impossible to toss back out into the cold.

Instead of driving to the front door when she was finished with her visits, therefore, Bess took the carriage directly to the stables. There she saw Bradford's son being tormented by an older boy, one of the real grooms. Oh, he was Carroll's butter-stamp, all right, with that bright auburn hair gleaming in the sunlight as the larger boy held his knit cap out of reach. He had Joia's straight spine, Hollice's stubborn lip, Meredyth's silly ears, but he was all Bradford, including the unquenchable spirit in the face of greater odds. He couldn't reach his hat, but he could turn the air blue with his curses.

Lady Carroll climbed down from her carriage, unaided by the brawling boys, and marched over to where they were now scuffling on the ground. She snapped her riding whip in the air, getting their attention in a hurry. The groom hung his head, sure his days of employment were over. He was hardly more than a child himself, Bess knew, and his family needed his salary. Snatching the now dusty knit cap out of his hands, she ordered him to take her horse and rig to the head groom. "I won't report your behavior to Jake yet," she told him with a glare, "but if I ever see you picking on anyone smaller than yourself, I'll have you dismissed before you can blink twice."

Bess stuffed the cap down over the littler boy's head and grabbed a handful of his muddy shirt. "And you, sirrah, if I ever hear you using those words again, I'll wash your mouth out with soap. I do not know where you learned them, but they will not do for a gentleman's son, do you understand?"

Meanwhile and without conscious decision, she was dragging the child toward the house, away from the stable block.

"Yes, ma'am," the boy whimpered. "I didn't mean to cause no trouble. M'lord made me swear not to. But Freddy was calling me names. Bad names."

Bess looked down. "You are not crying, are you? Lord Carroll would not be proud of that either."

The boy raised his chin and swiped at the tears on his cheeks. "No, ma'am."

The countess reached in her pocket for a handkerchief, cursing her husband in language nearly as blasphemous as the boy's. The child had a bruise forming on his chin, and what appeared to be a fading black eye. He was underweight and undersized. Dear Lord, what had those savages been doing to the poor child? "Fine, see that you don't. You, sir, are no longer a groom. You'll have a room in the nursery until school resumes. I shall expect you to behave like a gentleman at all times while you are in my house. Do you understand?"

"Oh, yes, ma'am." He bobbed his head and looked up at her worshipfully. "My lady."

There were Meredyth's laughing green eyes and wide grin, with the front teeth missing. Oh, she'd murder Bradford for this, see if she didn't.

She wouldn't surrender, though. "Bartholemew, a distant connection of the family has come to stay awhile."

The butler nodded. Half-sized Carroll relatives were herded through the door by their shirtfronts every day, tracking dust and manure through the halls of Winterpark. "I'll see to his baggage, my lady."

Bess could see the old faker's lips twitching, but she would not give in. "He will be residing in the nursery until his—until Lord Carroll makes other arrangements. Please see that the rooms are made ready, and reassign one of the maids."

It was a good thing the mistress seldom had call to visit the nursery wing, Bartholemew thought, or she'd know he'd had the housekeeper turn the rooms out weeks ago. He bowed to the filthy little scrap who was clutching his cap in his hands and gazing about him in awe. "If you will follow me, Master Noel, I think you will find the accommodations to your liking."

Noel? the countess repeated to herself. Bradford had named the boy Noel? She'd kill him for sure.

Chapter Twenty-five

*T*here was a conspiracy at Winterpark. Everyone from the bootboy to the butler wanted the child to be accepted, it seemed to Bess. Cook wanted to discuss what should be served in the nursery, instead of the menus for the hunt party. The countess's own lady's maid, diligently sewing small shirts without being asked by Lady Carroll, wondered if he needed three or four, since little boys were notoriously hard on clothes. The new nursemaid thought she should discuss the boy's progress with the mistress daily. Should he be allowed out to play? When should he be permitted back on his pony, and must Jake be along?

Bess told them all to use their best judgment, to leave her alone, she knew nothing about boys. Besides, she was busy with her gardens. Young men seemed to sprout higgledy-piggledy, out of her control, whereas her flower beds could be weeded and pruned. Pests were not coddled, not by Lady Carroll in her wide straw hat and thick leather gloves. No, they were fenced out or dug out or washed out. Not one blade of grass grew beyond its borders, not one slug dared leave a slimy trail. If only she could keep her house so well ordered.

The second footman brought her outgrown boots, for Master Noel. Jake from the stables sent over a flute he had carved. The dairy maids delivered extra milk, now that a child was in the house again. But why, Bess wondered, why were they all showing such kindness to a misbegotten man-child?

The boy was nothing but a trespasser, an interloper. He shouldn't have been born, he shouldn't have been brought to Winterpark, he shouldn't have the household's approval. Was she the only one to comprehend the disgrace of his very existence?

Bartholemew placed the tray of sweet rolls next to her plate and answered her question with one of his own: "What disgrace would that be, my lady? It is unfortunate that milord's brother Jack's marriage was never recognized, having taken place in a Catholic church in France, the records being destroyed in the wars. Now that omission can be rectified, thankfully. How propitious that you and the master discovered the poor orphaned tyke before he was sent to the workhouse. There is no disgrace, I assure you, in taking in one's departed relative's grandchild. To the contrary, it is a fine and generous deed, what one would expect from my lord and my gracious lady."

"Coming too brown, Bartholemew. Do you mean to tell me that any of the servants believe that Banbury tale? I didn't think we employed such buffleheads."

The butler cleared his throat. "The son of a coal-heaver would be better than Oliver Carroll, if you'll pardon my saying so, my lady. The household will gladly swallow any prescription that cures that particular malady. The boy is a Carroll, and thus he is the hope of Winterpark."

"And the hope of everyone's continued employment if he succeeds to the earldom. I see."

"Not entirely, my lady. There are those on the staff who simply enjoy having children about the house, and those who wish to see Lord Carroll restored to his, ah, more temperate self. In addition, Master Noel is a bright, friendly lad, already well thought of for his own sake, as you'd see if you—"

"What are the odds, Bartholemew?"

"Pardon, my lady?"

"The odds, Bartholemew. What are the current odds of the boy staying in this house and being adopted to succeed my husband?"

"Fifty-fifty," the old butler reported sadly. Oliver Carroll wasn't fit to clean Winterpark's stalls, but he was preferable to the disharmony in this house. It fair broke an old man's heart to see his beloved master and mistress on the outs.

Lady Carroll stood up, with Bartholemew hurrying to pull her chair out. "Don't bet your pension, Bartholemew. He is not staying."

The next morning a pencil drawing was beside Lady Carroll's plate at breakfast. There was a house and a horse and some trees, unless those floating things were birds.

"From Master Noel, my lady," Bartholemew announced. "He asked me to deliver it. I thought it quite well done myself."

The countess glanced briefly at the paper again. "My girls were better at that age."

"The young ladies had the benefit of your instruction."

"You are wasting your breath, Bartholemew." But she did stop in the village to buy a set of colored chalks at the emporium. And a set of watercolors. If the boy was as bright as everyone said, he could figure them out for himself.

At luncheon Bartholemew informed Lady Carroll that Mr. Oakes, the village schoolmaster, had stopped by. "I believe he wished to discuss hiring a new instructor."

While she had a child upstairs in her very house, receiving no lessons, no schooling whatsoever? What a coincidence. "It won't wash, Bartholemew. I am not employing a tutor for the boy. He will be back at school before the cat can lick its ear. Find one of the maids or footmen to teach him his letters if you are so concerned."

Bartholemew bowed. "Yes, my lady, you have always made sure the *servants* could read."

That night when she came down to her solitary dinner, a small, bedraggled bouquet of wild asters was at her place. Bess didn't need to ask where the wildflowers had come from, for they were absolutely not from her gardens or greenhouses. Emotional blackmail, that's what it was. A conspiracy indeed, right down to Bradford staying away longer than necessary, she was certain. He could stay away until hell froze over before she tended his wild oats. Lady Carroll ignored the sad little nosegay and ate her soup.

* * *

Merry and Max arrived before Lord Carroll returned home. Now the countess had a different problem: how to keep the boy's presence secret from her most impressionable daughter. Bess repeated her orders to the nursery maid to make sure there was no misunderstanding. The boy was to stay abovestairs, taking his meals in his room. When he was taken out for fresh air and exercise, he was to use the back stairs, the rear door, the kitchen garden.

"Oh, then I s'pose I'd best fetch him from the stables, ma'am," the maid said, sinking into a curtsy and sinking Lady Carroll's hopes.

Three red heads were out in the paddocks, three red heads catching the boy's pony, mounting up, riding out, laughing. Meredyth was most likely showing Max her favorite parts of Winterpark and teaching the boy which trees to climb, which tenants to visit for gingerbread and cider.

When they returned, Lady Carroll took her daughter aside. "Meredyth, darling, I realize you mean well, befriending the boy, but do you think it's wise? He will be leaving for school soon, you know, and a different life."

"Mama, I understand this is hard for you, truly I do, but he's just a little boy. Nolly never did anything to harm anyone. Would you have him cooped up in the nursery for weeks on end, with no playmates, nothing to occupy his mind?"

"Heavens, darling, don't make him out to be an abandoned puppy you have to rescue! I bought him paints and made sure there were books and toys."

"There are dolls, Mama! Hundreds of fragile, fussy dolls."

Which she would have known, had Bess ventured to the nursery wing. "He is not here long enough for that to matter," the countess insisted. "And I do not think that you should encourage him to think otherwise, for he'll be disappointed. His birth is such that he will never be socially acceptable, and you only reflect poorly on your own breeding by befriending him."

"Mama, half of his blood is the same as mine."

"But none of it is mine."

Merry had no answer. She kissed her mother's cheek and went upstairs, where her husband and Nolly were reenacting the Peninsula campaign on the nursery floor, using all those expensive, overdressed porcelain dolls as soldiers.

Joia was even less help, when she and Comfort arrived. "I was appalled myself, at first, to think that Papa could have . . . that is, that there was a child. But hiding him away won't change the fact that he exists. And now I see how important having an heir is to a man." She blushed and folded her hands over her stomach.

"Oh, Joia, does that mean you are increasing? Your father will be so pleased! And I, also, of course! Just think, two grandchildren in one year."

"It's early days, Mama, but yes, I think so. Comfort is thrilled and insists it is a boy. His firstborn wouldn't dare be anything else."

"Your father thought so, too, every time." She recalled again how disappointed they both had been, despite adoring their infant daughters.

"Yes, well, now Papa can also have an heir he approves. Oliver won't do, you know, even if he weren't such a thatch-gallows. With Aubergine heaven knows where, he's not likely to have any children. He cannot get the marriage annulled, and divorce is too expensive, to say nothing of that scandal. So Noel is the last Carroll left in line. Would you see Winterpark revert back to the Crown?"

"Of course not, darling, but the boy is—"

"Whatever Papa tells people he is. It's a good story, Mama, for no one can say that Uncle Jack didn't have a French wife or a son who died after sending Nolly to England. There are no records and no one to challenge the boy's right to Papa's notice."

"There is no proof, either, no birth certificates, no baptismal records, no wedding lines or death notices. A bastard cannot be heir to an earldom."

Joia waved that aside. "Barty says Mr. Rendell knows people who can provide such documents, but he doesn't think they'll be necessary if you lend your countenance to the boy."

"What, am I supposed to perjure myself before the courts?"

"No, Mama, of course not. You just have to accept Noel as if he were Uncle Jack's grandson. Why wouldn't you take him in, raise him as your own, make him part of the family? It is your behavior, keeping Noel locked away like the skeleton in the family closet, that gives the lie to the story. The servants will begin to take their cue from you, and well you know it. Then poor Nolly will be ostracized as a bastard, and Papa will have to petition the courts to break the entail, or to devolve the title onto my firstborn son. But, Mama, my son won't be a Carroll. He'll be an Ellingsworth, and the next heir to the Duke of Carlisle."

"I cannot do anything about it, Joia."

"Of course you can. If you accept Nolly as Papa's legitimate heir, no one has to know otherwise."

Lady Carroll wiped her eyes, wishing she had her husband's larger square of linen instead of her own scrap of lace. That gudgeon Bradford was never in the right place, and now everything was Bess's fault. Not even this firstborn child, the flesh of her body and mirror image of her own youth, could understand. "If no one knew, Joia, if no one ever had the least suspicion, I would still know."

Chapter Twenty-six

*S*he was losing them all, her husband and now her daughters. Bess sat alone in her drawing room, which had used to ring with happy laughter and music. Now it was silent and empty, with only the crystal goblets to show that anyone had been here. Bartholemew hadn't come in to clear away the champagne from the toast at Joia's happy news. He was most likely upstairs in the nursery with everyone else.

Bradford had come home that afternoon, tired but satisfied that he had the problems of his Yorkshire property solved. "I am never leaving home again," he swore, sinking into a chair after the hugs and kisses of his daughters, the handshakes of his sons-in-law, and the frantic barking of Merry's dog. The countess knew they would have their own welcome, later, upstairs. She also knew, from the way the earl was watching Max like a hungry cat with its eyes on the milk bucket, that he would soon offer Merry's husband the position of estate manager. As well he should, Bess agreed, for, despite all her protests otherwise, Bradford was too old to go traipsing around the countryside. She could tell his rheumatics were paining him, and most likely his digestion, too, from eating inn fare without her to plan his meals. He *did* need her, Bess told herself, but not nearly as much as she needed him.

Then Joia had made her announcement. Years fell away from Carroll's lined cheeks, and his green eyes sparkled as he made the toasts over the champagne Bartholemew had waiting. "I suppose you'll take some fool notion into your head, Comfort, and insist the babe be born at Carlisle, eh? No matter. Bess and I shall be there, won't we, my love?"

"I thought you were never leaving home again, Bradford. If you've had a change of heart, we could go up to London with Joia after the house party. She means to enjoy one more Season, don't you, darling?"

They all laughed at how neatly the earl had been trapped, and then they related the latest news from Holly, from London, from the peace conference. Comfort reported on the progress of his Irish stud, and Max on his mangel-wurzels. One topic never came up in conversation, one name was never mentioned. The boy could have been sitting in the drawing room, though, Bess thought, his absence was such a tangible thing.

And then they all left. Joia thought she needed a nap, and Comfort saw her up the stairs. Merry decided Downsy needed a walk, but she and Max didn't leave the house. Bradford said he needed to freshen up after his journey, without the usual wink to Bess that invited her along for a private greeting. They were all gone to see the boy, of course.

Most of Bess's life had been dedicated to her family, to these walls of Winterpark. Now she felt like an outsider, a stranger, with nothing to show for her years of devotion. She wandered over to the mantel, where one of her husband's favorite paintings hung. It was a Lawrence he'd commissioned when the girls were younger. All three of them sat around their mother's skirts in what was supposed to be a gazebo, with flowers in the background. Joia held a bouquet, and Hollice a book. Little Meredyth played with a kitten in her lap.

On the opposite wall, a portrait of the earl was displayed. Bradford was portrayed, not in his youth, but with his dark red hair already showing silver at the temples. He was smiling, as if at the antics of his precious poppets across the room. Bess had never liked the painting, although her husband looked handsome and happy. He shouldn't have been alone, she always thought. There should have been a boy at his side.

* * *

"I cannot do it, Bradford," the countess said when her husband came to her bed late that night. She hadn't been waiting in their sitting room when he came upstairs, so he'd wandered into her chamber, candle in hand, fresh from his bath.

"If it's lovemaking you cannot do tonight, dear heart, I confess I'm glad, for I doubt I've the energy myself. May I join you, anyway? I'm deuced tired of sleeping alone, Bess. Lud, how I've missed you."

"And I, you, Bradford." She raised the bedcovers and moved over to give him room.

He blew out the candle and kissed her soft cheek. "I must really be growing old."

"Never, my love." She snuggled against him, breathing in the scent of his sandalwood soap, feeling his arms wrap her in his familiar strength. This was where she belonged, Bess thought, till death did them part, not when the past came between them. "But that's not what I cannot do."

"I know, dearest. I know." He kissed the top of her head, there on his chest, and stroked her back. "And I won't ask any more of you. Thank you for trying, and for taking the boy in while I was gone."

Guilt tore at her. "I didn't try, Bradford. I let the servants do everything for him. He would have been all alone if Merry hadn't come."

"Nonsense, my pet," he soothed. "All I heard about was how m'lady saved him from the bully in the stable yard. Anyone who stands up to young Freddy, it seems, is top of the trees."

"I would have done the same for a street urchin."

"But Nolly doesn't know that. And I know you never would have bought a set of paints for a ragamuffin who got into brawls. The boy is filling the nursery with paintings of his pony. So far they look more like brown clouds to me, but the lad is pleased as punch."

"He's most likely using too much water. The girls all did, at first."

Lord Carroll nodded, there in the dark. "I'll tell him."

Bess had always loved to listen to the rumble of Bradford's

voice, with her ear on his chest. "What else shall you tell him, about me?"

"That you are the best thing that ever happened to me. That when I was away I felt as if a part of me was missing."

"Am I that part, Bradford, truly?"

"The best part, my love, the very best. I'll tell him that I need you to myself, that I'm just a selfish old ogre who can't bear to share you with anyone else. I'll visit him at school, and perhaps he can come here for part of the summer. He'll understand."

He'd understand that he wasn't wanted. Bess tried not to think of a little boy's pain. "You would send him away, then, for me?"

"I won't send him to America, Bess, but I'll make sure he's gone from Winterpark. It was too much to hope that you'd take him under your wing. I never should have asked, my dear, I know that now. Soon you'll be too busy with the girls and your grandchildren anyway."

"Where will he go?" Bess wanted to know. It was one thing to wish the boy out of her sight, another to wish him unhappy. She was feeling remorseful enough without imagining him lonely and unfed, preyed upon by bigger boys. "You will not incarcerate him at a school until he is eighteen, like some felon, Bradford."

The earl chuckled and smoothed the long braid that trailed down her back. "No, I'll find another foster family for him, near the academy. Meantime Merry and Max have offered to keep him in Kent. They're going to go to London with Joia and Comfort after the house party, to look at some livestock on auction. I'll send Noel to them when they're back at their own place. Merry will claim him as a cousin."

Bess nodded. Meredyth was always claiming something to nurture.

Bradford was going on: "Joia wanted to have him, and her viscount agreed, but I couldn't see sending him to London."

"You couldn't see sending anyone to London, Bradford, where you might have to go visit. But you are right, it's no place for a child, especially not with Joia and Craighton so much in the social whirl. And then there is the baby coming.

The boy would be left at Carlisle House with no one to care for him but a parcel of London servants who are most likely more haughty than Carlisle himself."

They both knew how arrogant servants would treat a child of uncertain pedigree. "No, he'll be better with Merry," Carroll agreed. "She'll have the house filled with orphaned lambs and broken-winged sparrows. And Max will be a good influence, too. A young hero for him to look up to, that's what a boy needs."

A boy needed to be able to speak to women, too, Bess thought. But dear Maxwell was getting better, amongst the family, at least, and Merry never had the slightest difficulty expressing herself to anyone. "Oh dear, I do hope Meredyth doesn't teach him to be so outspoken. Or so careless of the proprieties." She frowned in the dark. "Or to be such a daredevil rider as she was as a youngster."

"I told you we shouldn't have taken mitten to Astley's Amphitheatre when she was still an infant, but you insisted we all go to London for that Season, too. How many limbs did she break before she learned to stand on her pony's back? Wasn't that the summer my hair turned white?"

Lady Carroll shuddered, remembering. "Let us hope that Maxwell has enough sense for all of them."

"He had enough wits to marry our girl, didn't he?" The earl sighed, the sound reverberating through Bess's cheek. "That's why I wanted the boy here, love. Not to upset you, but because I wouldn't have to worry about someone turning him into a madcap or a weakling or a misanthrope. You'd have done a good job of rearing him, while letting him find his own self. You did it with the girls and they couldn't have turned out better."

"You make it sound as if I raised our daughters all by myself, Bradford. You know I did no such thing, but had you by my side the whole time."

He laughed. "You know I would have spoiled them unmercifully if not for your good sense."

"But I would have tried to make them into pattern cards of respectability without your leavening influence."

"We were good parents, weren't we, my girl?"

"We were the best, dearest. And we'll be superb grand-parents, for we can overindulge the unmannerly little darlings to our hearts' content, then send them home to their unsuspecting parents. That should make up for some of the sleep we lost worrying over the girls."

The earl stroked her back while Bess listened to the steady rhythm of his heart. Before sleep claimed her, the most contented, restful sleep she'd had in weeks, Bess had to say, "I truly am sorry about the boy, Bradford."

"Shh, Bess. It's done."

"But what about meantime? What shall we tell the servants and the houseguests?"

"We'll tell the gabble-grinders that we're investigating the boy's parentage. With no proof coming out of France, we're not ready to press his claim. They'll understand. The highest sticklers will be pleased we aren't trying to foist a cuckoo bird into their nest without more research. And the servants won't expect a sprig in short pants to be invited among the company anyway."

"There will be talk."

"There will always be talk, my love. All you need do if one of the scandalmongers pries is look down your beautiful patrician nose and change the topic. That never fails to silence the worst gossips, Countess Carroll."

"Or you could raise one of your elegant eyebrows, Lord Carroll, and sneer. That deflates the pretensions of the most tenacious toadeaters."

"You see? We are a good combination, nearly invincible. And don't worry, Bess. The boy will be fine."

"But will you be fine, too, Bradford?"

"I will be, with you by my side. In fact, I don't feel quite so ancient tonight after all. What about you?"

Chapter Twenty-seven

*G*uilt was a lumpy mattress beneath Lady Carroll. That and her husband's snoring were keeping her awake. Bess could have pulled the pillow out from under his head, or tried to roll him over, but he'd likely wake then, and he needed his sleep. Bess needed to think. She carefully inched out of Bradford's embrace and off the bed, into her robe and slippers, all without lighting the candle until she reached the sitting room.

Instead of relighting the fire, though, or making herself comfortable on the sofa, the countess tiptoed out to the hall and up the stairs. Why was she skulking about? she asked herself, pausing on the landing. It was her house, after all.

She was mistress here, the keeper of vigils, the upholder of virtues—and the victor. She'd won. Her husband loved her enough to give up his own flesh and blood, his dreams of posterity, for her. Why did her triumph taste like coal dust on her tongue, then, bitter and making her eyes tear? Why did she feel so very small and unworthy of the great love he'd shown?

Bess found herself outside the nursery door. A lamp was burning, on her orders. Joia had been afraid of the dark—or was it Hollice?—and a little boy in a strange place might need the same security. She went past the playroom to the bedchamber, telling herself that she had to make sure she was doing the right thing, making Bradford send the boy away. She wasn't just acting out of stubborn pride over an old wound, she swore to herself, nor out of jealousy, fearful of sharing her husband's affection. No, she could not be that mean, that vengeful, that petty.

It was for the boy's sake, she maintained. He'd be better off elsewhere. Bess could let Noel stay on, but she could never love him, never treat him like one of her own, and he'd know. Children always did. No, it was far better to let him go to Merry, thence to a loving family, she told herself as she stood over the sleeping boy. She'd go along with Bradford to make sure they were decent, kind people who believed in education and art, honor and horses, for the Carroll part of him.

The auburn-haired lad looked to be all Carroll, by the dim glow from the other room. She couldn't recognize anything of a stranger about him as he lay on his back, thin arms flung to either side on top of the rumpled covers. Noel was not any plump and dimpled cherub, Bess could see, but was thin and wiry, more like Meredyth than either of her sisters. Bess tucked his hands in and smoothed the blankets, dislodging one of the priceless porcelain dolls. The doll's long hair had been lopped off—with a penknife, it appeared—and a rough uniform had been cobbled out of some red fabric. Surely those were Meredyth's uneven stitches, and surely the gold braid on the little doll-soldier's chest was the trim from her own parasol that Downsy had chewed last week. Tomorrow the boy would get real toy soldiers, Bess vowed, if she had to send to London for them.

She touched his soft cheek—only to see if he was warm enough—and brushed the tumbled tresses off his forehead. How he must hate those sweet girlish curls, she thought, and how short must they be trimmed before he returned to school, so none of the other boys teased him? Happily, he didn't have to worry about those freckles as a girl would have done. Then again, Meredyth never did, tossing her bonnet aside as soon as she was out of sight of the house. As if her mother couldn't tell the chit was sun-speckled more than ever. A loving mother always knew those things, and that was what Noel deserved.

Bess touched her fingers to her lips and then to the boy's forehead in farewell. She was doing the right thing. She could never love him. He snored.

The house party proceeded. The ladies exclaimed over the gardens, and the gentlemen enjoyed the stables, except for the duke, who dallied with Dora at the Carrolton Arms, so he was not a nuisance. The weather held for three fine days of sport.

Joia didn't ride out with the hounds, blushingly citing her condition. Merry didn't go either, declaring that if she couldn't wear breeches, she wouldn't enjoy the hunt. She spent the time with Noel instead, schooling him on his pony or teaching him to do handstands. Joia took him sketching. Watercolor paintings appeared regularly with Lady Carroll's breakfast tray. Cook claimed Master Noel for an hour in the morning, ostensibly to teach him French, but more likely to fatten him up on strawberry tarts and syllabub, the countess suspected. Bartholemew let him help in the butler's pantry, educating him in the Carroll family history with every silver heirloom they polished.

When the gentlemen returned, Max played war games in the nursery, and Comfort played jackstraws. Both couples together taught the boy archery, billiards, and cricket, with much laughing and shouting. Lord Carroll watched from the window, a melancholy smile on his face. Bess was right: he was too old to play father to the little scamp.

And Lady Carroll pretended Noel was not there.

None of the guests commented, for there was nothing in the boy's presence to stir the scandalbroth. A connection of the earl's late brother, eh? Every noble family had relatives of dubious descent, so what? The wine was excellent, the food delicious, and the brat was behind closed doors. The Carrolls were kind enough not to subject their guests to a child's prattling or plunking on the pianoforte or poetry recitation, unlike most houses where the youngsters were paraded around like prize pullets. A toast to the host and hostess.

The countess simply smiled.

When the company left, family and guests alike, Lord Carroll started taking Noel about with him again, on horse and pony-back or beside him in the curricle. They went to visit the tenants, to check the fields, and to make sure Rendell Hall was ready for its owners—and for the earl's first grandchild.

Bess didn't begrudge the boy the time with his father now that she knew he'd be leaving soon. And she didn't miss her girls as badly, knowing they'd return for Christmas. Hollice would, too. Lady Carroll kept busy cleaning up her flower beds before winter and sewing infant dresses before the grandbabies were born.

The crisp fall weather of the hunt party gave way to cold, raw days with chilling rains that made the earl's bones ache. As he fell into bed each night the earl complained—but only to himself—that indefatigable small boys were hell on old men.

Then Merry's letter came, saying she and Max were returned to Kent. Should they come fetch Noel? And did he want a pet turtle? Carlisle's niffy-naffy French chef was going to make soup out of this one, so Merry had borrowed it. Perhaps she and Max could stay at Carroll House in Grosvenor Square during their next visit to London.

The earl decided to deliver Noel himself. Bradford said he wanted to go to see the new livestock and how Max was managing his property. Bess believed he wanted to spend a few more days with the boy, so chose not to go along. She supervised the packing of Noel's trunk while the boy and the earl took one last jaunt about the countryside the day before departing. Bess made sure the nursery maid packed Noel's paints and soldiers and books, as well as his meager supply of clothes. If she knew her daughter, the boy would come home muddied every day. He'd need additional changes of clothing, so Bess made a quick trip to the village to purchase more shirts and stockings, another heavy jacket. That afternoon while they were yet out riding, she raided the pantry and the still room and even her lord's wine cellar, filling a hamper for Merry.

By teatime, the countess ordered water heated for baths. They'd be chilled, and Bradford would be creaking louder than Prinny's corsets.

While she dressed for dinner, Bess fretted. It wasn't like the earl to worry her unnecessarily, or to miss his meal. He wouldn't have absconded with his son to avoid the separation, so he must have run into some difficulty. One of his precious horses must have come up lame or something. A messenger would be arriving soon, she was confident.

"Hold dinner," she told Bartholemew, and started pacing in front of the windows. So it was that the countess was the first to see the small figure limping along the carriage drive in the dusk. No messenger, no horse, only Noel. "My God," she cried, flying for the door.

Also on the watch, the head groom and Jem Coachman were already there when she reached the boy, Bartholemew wheezing behind her. The two stable men and their assistants were surrounding the child, shouting questions at him. Noel was sobbing.

"Stop this, all of you!" the countess commanded. "Can't you see you are frightening the boy worse?" They all fell back, giving her room to kneel in the muddy lane and put her hands on the boy's soaked jacket, feeling his thin body trembling beneath. "Hush, Noel, you know his lordship doesn't like crying. You have to tell us what happened, so we can go help him." She unwrapped her shawl and placed it over his slim shoulders.

Noel hiccuped and nodded, gulped and wiped his nose on the back of his wet sleeve. "We went to the old Mahoney place, to see if Merry and Max might like living there or if it'd been deserted too long. Then m'lord said he knew a shortcut back."

Jem groaned. "There be five lanes through the woods." The countess gave him a lowering look until he subsided so the boy could go on.

"And m'lord said I could hold the ribbons." More moans and a few curses, one from Lady Carroll. "He said you'd be mad."

"But not at you, darling. Go on."

"A deer ran out, right in front of the horses, and . . . and the horses bolted and the carriage overturned and m'lord is under it and I couldn't lift it. I tried, my lady, I swear I tried!"

He was sobbing again, so Bess wrapped him in her arms and rocked him back and forth, even though her own heart was breaking. "I'm sure you did, Noel, I'm sure. But what then? He spoke to you? He was awake?" And alive, she prayed.

Noel bobbed his head again. "He told me to unhitch the horses and ride for help. Castor was limping," he said with a fearful look at Jake, "but his leg wasn't broke. And Pollux didn't like anyone on his back, but I got a fistful of his mane in my hand. M'lord pointed which way to go, and said the horse would find his way home. But it started to rain again and my fingers got cold and Pollux didn't like the trees so close. I . . . I fell off. You won't tell Merry, will you?"

"Meredyth fell off many a time herself, Noel, but I won't tell. How did you get home, then? Did you pass someone who went back for Lord Carroll?"

Noel shook his head. "No one came, and there were no houses. I walked and walked and then it got dark."

"You poor boy, alone in the woods. You must have been very frightened."

He looked surprised. "No, ma'am. I climbed a tree, is what, the tallest I could find, and I saw the lights." He pointed behind her, at the four stories of Winterpark, candles burning in half its windows.

Bess kissed his forehead and nudged him toward Bartholemew. "Take Master Noel inside and see he is warm and dry, as soon as you send someone for the doctor. I want every manservant who can sit a horse out front in five minutes, with lanterns. Jem, we'll need a carriage to bring his lordship home, but that will have to follow as fast as you can. I want my mare saddled first."

Everything was already being done, of course, but Bess needed to make sure.

Jake was shouting orders to his grooms, cursing. "We'll have to start at Mahoney's and divide up, followin' every one of those blasted paths. Be deuced hard to find 'em in the dark, too."

"I can find the right one from this side, through the woods," a small voice spoke up. "I left markers."

"What a brave, clever boy you are," Bess told him. "Let's

get you into dry clothes and then you'll ride with me on my mare to find your . . . Lord Carroll."

"Pardon, m'lady," Jake put in. "Every minute counts. I'd never forgive m'self for leavin' 'is honor out in the woods under the rig a second longer'n necessary."

"And he would never forgive me, nor I myself," Bess said, headed back toward the house, the boy's hand in hers, "for letting his son catch his death of pneumonia."

Chapter Twenty-eight

Two broken ribs, a collapsed lung, and a twisted knee were nothing compared to what Lady Carroll was going to do to her husband when he woke up, for giving her such a fright. She hadn't left his side since they found him unconscious under his curricle two days ago. The doctor pronounced him out of danger, unless the congestion in his chest worsened. Bess had every herb in the still room brewed and ready. She sat by his bedside listening to his every breath for signs of peril or improvement. Her sewing was in her hands, but prayers were on her lips.

The earl stirred restlessly and Bess dropped the infant gown to feel his forehead, to hold his hand.

"Bess, is that you, my love?"

"Who else did you think would be here, you old fool?" She tried not to weep, knowing how he hated her tears.

"Saint Peter, actually." He spoke in a raspy voice, then gripped her hand harder. "The boy?"

"He is fine, Bradford, don't worry. You should be proud of such a brave child. Now, go back to sleep. You need your rest."

The earl couldn't rest yet. "He is a fine lad, isn't he, Bess? You'll look after him for me, won't you? I know you'll do right by him, I can trust you."

"Of course you can trust me, you looby. I wouldn't put the reins of a high-strung pair into the hands of a little boy."

He nodded and tried to smile. "My love. Now I'm ready for Saint Peter."

"Nonsense. I shall not have you talking that way, Bradford. You'll be here for many a long year to come because that boy needs you, and I need you. Besides, I am already planning Noel's wedding. It's to be the grandest affair London has ever seen. I might even rent all of Vauxhall Gardens if you aren't around to complain. You owe me that wedding, Bradford."

But the earl's eyes were already drifting closed.

"Will he die, Lady Bess?" Noel had finally been allowed in to see the earl. Everyone had been whispering for days, though, so he feared the worst as he beheld the white-haired man, so pale in the huge bed.

Bess brushed the red curls back from Noel's forehead, where a bruise was fading. "No, darling, he's just sleeping. He's too stubborn to die and I'm too stubborn to let him. Besides, you saved his life, remember?"

"I did, didn't I?" He turned to her, all freckled smiles. Then his grin faded. "If m'lord isn't dying, why are you weeping? He doesn't like it, you know." He fumbled through his pockets for the handkerchief Barty had insisted he carry. "Here." He offered it to Lady Carroll. "Mine is bigger'n yours."

"And your heart is, too, precious." She lifted him onto her lap in the chair next to the earl's bed. "But that is going to change."

Noel leaned back against her, content in her warmth and comfort as he'd never been in his memory. "I am too old for this, you know," he said sleepily a minute later.

Bess kissed the top of his head. "So am I, darling, but we'll both have to suffer."

They wouldn't let the earl out of bed, to his outrage. "Who is going to look after my horses, my investments, my tenants?" he bellowed.

"Meredyth and Sir Maxwell, Hollice and Mr. Rendell, and Joia and Viscount Comfort, in that order. Quite capably, too, my dear." Lady Carroll was at his bedside, as usual, with her sewing. "One or the other of them is here reporting to you every minute, so it's no wonder you aren't getting enough rest. And shouting won't help you recuperate any faster, my love."

He plucked at the bedclothes. "But what about the boy?"

"What, did you think the girls would leave him alone for an instant after he rescued their papa? Noel is as busy as a fox in the henhouse. I could have saved the effort of hiring him a tutor, for all the man sees of the boy."

"But it's nearly Christmas and I haven't done any shopping."

"The girls need nothing, now that their husbands are indulging them, and if it's the boy you are worried about, you'd do better to worry that they are spoiling him past redemption. I've never seen so many toy soldiers, miniature swords, games and puzzles and books, in my life." And that wasn't including the pile of gifts she'd purchased for him.

The earl took her hand. "But what about you, my dear? I've been a sore trial to you, I know. I would get you a gift to make up for that."

She raised his hand to her lips. "Having you and my family together at Christmas is the best present I could ask for. If I'd lost you . . ." She couldn't finish. "And you, what do you want for Christmas, Bradford?"

"Your love is all I've ever wanted, Bess."

"I know, dearest, and you have it, forever."

On Christmas morning Lord Carroll insisted on holding the morning prayers in Winterpark's own chapel, as the earls of Carroll had done since the family's beginnings. He walked, slowly to be sure, and on the arms of two of his handsome sons-in-law, to the front of the small chapel, to the chair that had been placed there, the Bible beside it. He saw that the servants were already assembled in the far pews, along with a small handful of houseguests. In the front sat his daughters and their husbands, Holly big with child, Joia with a Madonna-like glow, and Merry grinning with her own supposedly secret news. The earl and Bartholemew were already making book on another little soldier.

Bess hadn't come yet, but it was Christmas. She had a hundred things to do. And the boy was likely with his tutor. Bradford sighed. He had so much, his heart was so full, he wouldn't wish for the moon. He started to read the Christmas story, as heads of households all across England were reading it that morning.

Toward the middle he heard a latecomer arrive. Without lifting his head, he knew it was his Bess, the way he always knew when she entered a room. He kept reading.

"Well, I never!" he heard the Duchess of Carlisle exclaim.

And Bess answered, "No, and that's why you see your son but twice a year. I'm surprised Comfort turned out as well as he did."

Now the earl looked up, to see his beloved wife take the very front seat in the chapel, light from the stained-glass windows casting a reflected rainbow on her—and on the boy by her side in the family pew. Bess straightened Noel's neckcloth and placed her arm around his shoulder.

It didn't matter that tears blurred the page in front of him, Lord Carroll knew the words by heart: "And lo, unto them that day a son was born. . . ."

On sale now!

*From an exciting new voice in romantic fiction comes
this powerful tale of two souls bound by cruel destiny.*

NIGHT IN EDEN
by Candice Proctor

Sentenced to a life of servitude in New South Wales
for a crime she did not commit, Bryony Wentworth
is ready to fight for her life. Wanting no part of the
man who would save her, the rugged and enigmatic
Captain Hayden St. John, Bryony suppresses the passion that threatens to overwhelm her.

Set against the panorama of a harsh, gorgeous, and
unforgiving land, this passionate pair learns to trust,
to love, and to triumph over the danger that shadows
their lives until destiny and desire become one.

On sale now!

*In Regency England, there is a very thin line between
love and hate and betrayal . . .*

ENTWINED
by Emma Jensen

Nathan Paget, Marquess of Oriel, returns to London
society a great military hero of the Peninsular Campaign
and a most eligible bachelor. Unbeknownst to the rest of
the world, Nathan has been blinded and has only one
goal in mind—to uncover the traitor responsible for the
death of his comrades and for his injury. He shares his
secret with only one person, the headstrong and beautiful
Isobel MacLeod, who agrees to serve as his "eyes" and help
him unmask the traitor in their midst. This unlikely duo
can barely stand each other's company—or so they think
until they find themselves falling deeply in love, a love
threatened by an unknown enemy with murder and
betrayal in his heart.

Published by Ballanntine Books.
Available in your local bookstore.

Love Letters

Ballantine romances are on the Web!

Read about your favorite Ballantine authors and upcoming books on our Web site, LOVE LETTERS, at **www.randomhouse.com/BB/loveletters**, including:

♥What's new in the stores
♥Previews of upcoming books
♥In-depth interviews with romance authors and publishing insiders
♥Sample chapters from new romances
♥And more . . .

Want to keep in touch? To subscribe to Love Notes, the monthly what's-new update for the Love Letters Web site, send an e-mail message to **loveletters@cruises.randomhouse.com** with "subscribe" as the subject of the message. You will receive a monthly announcement of the latest news and features on our site.

So follow your heart and visit us at **www.randomhouse.com/BB/loveletters!**